D1522806

RETURN TO "SUNSET HOUSE"

Also available in this series:

RETURN TO "SUNSET HOUSE"

THE CONTINUATION OF "BEAUTY FOR ASHES"

Lady Fortescue

ISIS
LARGE PRINT
Oxford, England

Copyright © 1948 Lady Fortescue

First published in Great Britain 1948
by William Blackwood & Sons Ltd

Published in Large Print 1997 by ISIS Publishing Ltd,
7 Centremead, Osney Mead, Oxford OX2 0ES,
by arrangement with Mrs Faith Grattan

British Library Cataloguing in Publication Data
Fortescue, Winifred, Lady, 1888-1951
    Return to "Sunset House": The continuation of Beauty for
    ashes. – Large print ed.
    1. Fortescue, Winifred, Lady, 1888-1951 2. Large type
    books 3. Provence (France) – Social life and customs
    4. Provence (France) – Social conditions
    I. Title
    944.9'082'092

ISBN 0-7531-5051-4

Printed and bound by Hartnolls Ltd, Bodmin, Cornwall

I dedicate this book to my readers all over the world.

Winifred Fortescue.

CHAPTER
ONE

Doodles

The long-awaited D-day came, with all its danger and glory of achievement; and then Hitler launched his secret weapon V1, the damnable Doodle.

I was lying in bed in the studio bedroom of "Many Waters" in perfect peace, with Dominie snoozling, for once in his basket, when he suddenly awoke, padded nervously across the moonlit room, reared up on his hind legs and put his head out of the window. Then he threw it back and let forth the most heart-rending howl. He was not in love at the moment, and no sound from outside accounted for this hair-raising noise. So I ordered him rather irritably to stop it. He looked at me apprehensively, again sniffed the outer air and repeated the performance. A chill ran down my spine; for this was abnormal behaviour, and I realised that he was trying to warn me of he knew not what.

Perhaps four minutes later I heard the queerest sound in the far distance, rather like the exhaust of a gigantic motor bicycle — the sound that always sent The Blackness mad. It approached with terrifying swiftness. Devoured by curiosity, I leaped out of bed and took my place beside Dominie at the open window, holding his stiff and trembling little body with my arm.

Then IT roared overhead. A queer devilish aeroplane, whizzing undeviatingly through space, shooting forth lurid flames from its tail. Somehow I realised that this was something new and evil and not one of our planes set on fire by enemy shells and seeking a landing place. The whole of my room seemed to vibrate with HATE. I collected The Blackness and, shivering as he did, I crept back to bed. Throughout the night these hellish machines crossed my cottage by two different routes from the coast, obviously making for London. I was certain that this must be the nice little surprise that Hitler had been designing for so long. The V1.

This was the arrival of the Doodle Bug — the name given, I believe, to these pilotless aircraft by the Americans. Pilotless? Why, I had SEEN the devil with horns and hooves driving them, and FELT the hate with which they were launched to kill as many of those cursed English as possible and destroy the nerves of the rest. Experts gave us advice about our behaviour when the engines of these devilish Doodles stopped overhead. One had exactly fifteen seconds in which to take cover. (If in an upstairs bedroom like mine there wouldn't be time to get anywhere. In that case it was suggested that one should crouch in a kneeling position, so that there was space around one. If lying on the stomach there was danger of being lifted into the air by blast and dropped again with force enough to burst one's inward pipes.) Charming device. The newspapers were reticent about the damage that had been done, but friends in London told us that it was terrible.

One never got accustomed to these nightmare

machines, though we heard that our airmen and anti-aircraft gun crews found great sport in trying to shoot them down as they flew at incredible speed. They preferred it to the night bombing of towns, for in destroying Doodles they did not kill men — and perhaps women and children. But the civilians loathed and feared them far more than any of the other horrors they had already suffered.

Only one stopped its engine immediately over my cottage, and on that night I shot out of bed, dragging The Blackness with me, and went into the little corridor where there were no windows, shutting my door behind me. I crouched in a kneeling position as advised by the experts, but of course the space in front of me was filled with Dominie. I muttered my usual good night to him, which was always, "You take care of me and I'll take care of you and God will take care of us both," made the sign of the Cross over him and myself — all very swiftly done — and slowly counted fifteen, wondering what it would be like on the Other Side — nicer than *this* at any rate.

When I had counted fifteen I was surprised to find that we were still alive. I counted twenty–thirty–forty. . . . In the end we both got sick of crouching in that chilly passage, went back to our bedroom and peered out of the window. A clear star-strewn sky. Nothing to be seen. After a while came a distant explosion which shook our doors and windows and made Dominie bark. Our Doodle was the very latest variety of Doodle designed to stop its engine, perhaps several times, and then glide on before the hellish machine made its final devastating dive.

In this way many thousands of people might have their nights wrecked after a hard and often dangerous day's work, and their nerve eventually destroyed. Only a mad brain could have devised such subtle torture.

The V2 when it came to London did incredible damage, but people — not near the explosions — living in London minded them far less than the Doodle Bugs, because they were noiseless bombs falling from the stratosphere, and you were either dead or you weren't. There was no warning and no horror of anticipation. All the same, if they had begun earlier — or gone on longer — what would have happened to poor London?

CHAPTER
TWO

France is Freed

On the day that France was liberated and Paris freed rain was pouring from leaden skies, a dim, sad day. I had turned on the wireless at intervals since morning, for the whole world was tense with expectation, and at last I was rewarded for my vigilance and heard the glorious news followed by the playing of The Marseillaise. I sprang to my feet and stood at attention filled with a proud joy too deep for description. I could picture the mad rejoicings in Paris, and knew what balm it would be to the lacerated feelings of the French that the Parisians had helped to liberate themselves.

Then further realisation came — Elisabeth was not there to welcome our invading army, she whose faith in our ultimate victory had never faltered. In all her letters she had said: "Come soon! Time is so long." It was too long. . . . Now, at last, I could go home — but she would not be there. A great wave of bitterness engulfed me, and I sank into my chair and hid my face in my arms upon my desk. The Blackness became frantic. He reared up on his hind legs and with little whimpering cries tried to force his nose close to my face. Then I had to comfort *him*.

I walked to the window overlooking the rain-soaked

valley, my mind now filled with tragic thoughts of Elisabeth's martyrdom. And then above the sodden woods, suddenly, once more, I saw her. She was dancing joyously in a field starred with every flower in the world, lovelier than those of the mountain slopes of the High Alps in spring. She was carrying a tricolour flag, and as she danced she waved it in the air, then pirouetted madly and pointed a slender bare toe towards a narcissus. She was joy personified. Her great eyes blazed with excitement, the unruly lock of hair which always tumbled over her brow tossed in the breeze, her little white teeth gleamed. Then she looked straight at me, pointed the flag towards France, and cried, "Pegs! COME ON!"

No, I didn't imagine it. I was thinking of her lovely body marred and tortured, that slender frame starved to emaciation and the great eyes filled with the patient anguish of physical pain and mental frustration, loneliness and longing. And for the second time since she went over to the Other Side I had seen her LAUGHING among flowers.

Before she fell ill we had heard that she had consented to serve on the Relief Committee for the children of our area, working with the Quakers and acting as representative of the American Red Cross. It came to me at this moment, prompted surely by her mind, that when I returned to France I must continue her work. I decided to tell French Headquarters that now that Sussex was organised and France liberated I would henceforth make appeal for the children of Provence. This was the decision I made on the day of the liberation of France.

CHAPTER
THREE

The Great Response

It is very hard to fight fiercely and incessantly to achieve something you dread; to battle with formalities and departments; to suffer disillusion and discouragement: to struggle on towards a goal, knowing that if — and when — you reach it you will find loneliness and heartbreak. For a year I did this, working night and day for the sick and starving children of Provence, raising a fund in memory of — "Mademoiselle" — my beloved companion.

Without the inspiration of her presence, her originality, artistry and fun, life on our lovely little mountain in Provence was almost unimaginable, and unbearable to think of, yet I knew that she wanted me to go back and to carry on the work she was doing. Even when most dunched by blocked avenues and broken hopes, I felt the spur of her vital personality pricking me on to fresh endeavour.

All I could do to get money for HER fund was to appeal to all the kind people from all over the world who had written me about my books, and they responded magnificently. This present book, which had only reached Chapter VII, had to be laid aside while

I wrote letters and sent out appeals till one-thirty and two a.m. I know now how an expectant mother unable to deliver her child must feel — VERY restless and uncomfortable. Alas, I never had a baby, but I think that producing a book must be very like creating a child. The only difference would seem to be that an author has not the compensation of surprise at the end — girl? — or boy? She knows all about her offspring before it is born.

Well, I had been experiencing labour of a different kind, but it brought forth much fruit, and the enthusiasm with which the schools and convents of England to whom I appealed backed my crusade was very lovely. They showered sacks of little garments, shoes, medicaments and comforts upon me, all of which were packed and actually exported before the dockers' strike.

In my appeal I had pleaded not only for money but for gifts in kind, even if it were only a packet of needles, a reel of thread, a cake of soap, a bandage — for everything is precious to those who have NOTHING.

I had not dreamed that the response would be so immediate. Parcels containing clothes, shoes, soap, mending materials, toys, medical and surgical supplies, and innumerable other things were dragged down the precipice to my door by the good-natured postwoman, and then I realised that when the day came for my removal from "Many Waters" all these things must be packed and dragged up that terrible slope again. I must try to find a room in the village where they could be received, sorted, packed and stored ready for shipment. One of the great men of the neighbourhood, a builder by trade, a Rotarian with high ideals, immediately gave me the use of a room over his office, and one of his secretaries consented to unpack the parcels and make a list of the names and addresses of senders; for I was already overworked with ceaseless correspondence and could not visit the depôt every day. After the first week a telephone message urged me to come, because already there was hardly room to enter the store-room, which was piled to the ceiling with parcels and sacks. How wonderful! How inspiring and how heart-warming to find that this lone crusader had so many unknown friends so eager to help her to give aid to those pathetic children, eighty per cent of whom I had heard were suffering from rickets, skin diseases and gastric trouble from malnutrition.

Obviously the only thing to do was to start sorting and packing at once, storing the filled packing-cases elsewhere — my kind friend the builder would surely give me a corner in one of his sheds, and I was certain that some of the members of the Village Institute would help me with the sorting and packing.

Every one I asked was ready and willing to help, even if they could give only spot-labour a few hours weekly fitted in between war jobs, housework, queueing for food and cooking for a family — but the work these gallant women put in when they did come was quite extraordinary, bless them.

Of course I found that I was up against every kind of Government formality — my fund must be registered as a war charity, every plank of wood needed to construct the packing-cases, which I had decided to have made the size of children's cots so that the wood could be used in a country where planks could not be found, must be prayed for to a Government rightly bent on rebuilding bombed houses. My big builder nobly filled in all the many forms for me, and with his influence obtained wood. His dear carpenter made it up into strong cases — and then we found that they were too large to be carried up into my store-room! Nothing for it but to leave them piled one upon another in his already overcrowded carpentry shed, carry the clothes, soap, shoes, etc., down the stairs, across a big yard, and then climb the mountain of cases and fill the top one. I bought strong mattress-covers, striped buff and blue and rose, for both single and double beds. When the clothes were sorted into heaps — women's, girls', boys', babies' — we tied them into bundles, put them into the mattress-covers, and two of us would then stagger across the yard. We leaped or climbed over objects in the carpentry shed — tables, cupboards and *coffins* (I begged the carpenter to reserve the longest one for me, as I should surely need it soon) — we then packed the contents of the sacks into the top case, one of us having climbed the pile, balanced precariously while the other handed up bundles to be packed. All this to the soothing accompaniment of busy buzz-saws, hammering and filing — a din so great that one could hardly hear oneself speak.

Another dear friend of mine, the grocer and universal provider next door, supplied me with strong tea chests in which to pack tins.

In Lewes, when I was wandering in the High Street before addressing a meeting, I saw things displayed in the window of a big drapery store marked "coupon free" which would be precious in Provence. I went in, and told my story to an attractive, golden-haired directress. She was instantly sympathetic, and very soon enlisted the interest of her shop assistants, who ran this way and that, untiringly pulling out boxes and climbing up ladders to bring me oddments, slightly shop-soiled goods and pre-war stock. I asked if these things could be held for me, and the manager then offered empty rooms on the first floor; he even offered to provide me with an office should I need it. He flatly refused to allow me to pay any rent whatsoever, and the girls of that shop are still working for me.

Never had woman so many eager and helpful allies; but of one thing I am very sure, never was woman more grateful for such wonderful backing, and seldom can woman have needed friendly encouragement more before starting on a lone adventure.

CHAPTER
FOUR

The Great Adventure

There came the moment — in May of 1945 — when the French Authorities invited me to go to France to see for myself the conditions in the South and to find out the possibilities — and impossibilities — of doing immediate relief work. They knew, even better than I, the difficulties: lack of food and of every commodity because of lack of transport. In Southern Provence we make only wine, oil and perfume. Normandy was our larder, and with no trains or lorries or ships, the lovely butter and meat cannot be brought south.

The dreaded moment had come, but there were still more formalities ahead of me before I could start. I had no less than five invitations from important French organisations and a pressing one from the Mayor of Grasse, a clever doctor much distressed by the increase of tuberculosis among the children. But even so, I had to get the permission of the English Foreign Office to travel, and after that a formal authorisation and then a serial number before I could take my railway ticket.

Having heard of the fantastic prices in France, I was secretly appalled when I was informed that I was allowed to take with me only £5 of English money to get me to the port of embarkation, and £10 in French currency, just 2,000 francs. I should have to stay a night or two in Paris to see the French Red Cross, L'Entr'aide and other official bodies, and I had heard of the horrors of black market prices. Surely this simple old sheep would be shorn of even that which she had! And after that — the journey to the Midi; for it was not then possible, as in the luxurious days of old, to ask dear Mr. Cook to do all the work, and then just call for tickets booked through to one's destination.

I did not then know that I could make arrangements with my bank whereby, in France, I could replenish my purse. And so, as usual, I just trusted to *le bon Dieu* to get me out of any little — or big — difficulty that might arise, and, as you will see — HE DID.

So many delays had I suffered that at last a terrible resignation settled upon my restless spirit. So often had I telephoned to various offices and embassies to know if visas and permits and serial numbers had come through — and they never had — that I almost became a lady of leisure. I exercised my Blackness in the woods, and watched him plunge into the lakes and swim around like a baby hippo; and one day I arranged to have a day in London when I would do some shopping and have my grey curls shampooed and made *chic* by the coiffeur and friend who has tended them since they were golden-brown.

I went to London, and having had luncheon in the little restaurant of another old friend, I suddenly thought that I might as well ring up the Foreign Office again and find out at what date in the distant future I might expect my permit and serial number to be issued.

"You start to-morrow. Ten o'clock boat train from Victoria," came the shattering response to my enquiry.

"It can't be done," I babbled. "I'm here in London. I shall have to get back to Sussex and pack — then come up to London again. Having waited so long, surely you can arrange to give me longer notice?"

"I am afraid that if you don't take this opportunity you may not get another for months," came the inexorable reply, then, a more human postscript, "though I agree that it does seem a bit hard to keep you waiting so long, and then give you only a few hours' notice."

It certainly did. My hair, in so much need of my friend's attention, now stood on end. Positively I could feel my Chasseur Alpin beret rising with it. I rushed into his shop breathlessly to cancel my appointment, and then started pounding my way down to the first bus-stop for Victoria.

The rest of that day — and night — were a whirl and a nightmare collecting the 15 lbs. of food allowed for a month's visit to a hungry country, packing clothes, making foolproof lists of things to be done and letters to be written for the crusade in my absence, telephoning tradesmen to stop the milk, the meat, the rations until further orders, leaving cheques for bills; all the hundred and one things one must do personally. Finally, a long memorandum of DO'S and DON'TS on the subject of care of The Blackness while I was away — the tummy to be dried when he came in from bathing, the charcoal biscuit reward for good behaviour, the combing of silken ears and all the comforting he would need. (This last memorandum quite unnecessary, for he was to be left in the care of two devoted adopted aunts, else I never could have left him.)

It seemed hardly worth while going to bed at all when at last all these duties were finished. But as one of The Blackness's aunts had made the brilliant suggestion that instead of the bother of going up to London again encumbered with baggage, she should drive me straight to the port — Newhaven — only an hour's drive from the cottage, I could start later and have a few hours of sleep first.

We didn't have a puncture. We arrived in good time. The cross-Channel passage was calm, and I snoozed in my berth all the way. I got a corner seat in the Paris train at Dieppe, having soared triumphantly through the customs without having my modest baggage examined, just chalked without query. It gives one such a warm glow of satisfaction down one's spine to know that one's face is deemed to be honest.

In my carriage were a French naval officer, a French war correspondent and a French lady with a bright little boy, Jean Claude. I listened to their comments about England and life in England with much secret amusement. The lady declared: *"J'ai une admiration folle pour les Anglais — mais je ne les aime pas."* The naval officer, who (we afterwards learned) had travelled only around the suburbs of London on his one day's leave from his ship, found the English gardens *"tordant,"* all in rows and exactly alike with their little rockeries, and rose pergolas and squares of green grass.

Jean Claude, having spent his war years in safe security, always sure of his milk, his orange juice and good English food, was far more tolerant of us. Indeed he seemed to anticipate with some apprehension the return to the land of his birth.

To my amazement, a waiter in a white coat (nearly white) passed down the corridor ringing a bell and yelling *"Première Service."* Actually a restaurant car already reinstated where a succession of four luncheons were served — at a price. Forewarned, I had a good supply of sandwiches and hot coffee in a thermos flask; I need not budge.

The French war correspondent had fled after the waiter, and soon returned with five reserved seats for the luncheon car. One of these he handed, with a bow, to me. I thanked him warmly, but confessed that I was scared of French prices, and preferred to eat my sandwiches where I was.

Madame, with Jean Claude and followed by the French naval officer, filed out into the corridor, but the war correspondent lingered. When alone with me he made another beautiful bow and begged me to be his guest for luncheon. It would be such a happiness and privilege, he said, to be permitted, even in such a small way, to return some of the wonderful hospitality and kindness he had always received in my country. I remained firm, but I was deeply touched, especially as the boy's cuffs were frayed and his carefully polished shoes patched. I feared he would get a nasty jar when the bill for his luncheon was presented to him, and, as it afterwards transpired, he did. My fellow travellers came back with only semi-filled tumpkins, and the expression on their faces both sour and sad. I had fared better with my good beef and tomato sandwiches washed down with REAL coffee.

At every station we passed it was sad to see rows and rows of derelict railway carriages covered with the rust of years, the glass of windows gone, gaping squares where once were doors. Out of a total of 22,000 locomotives in France, the Germans had taken all but 2,000, leaving useless all these coaches. The waste of war!

The French Authorities in London had told me that my train would arrive at Gare St-Lazare at night. Accordingly I had sent a telegram to the kind unknown friend of a friend who had generously offered to house me while in Paris, telling her this and begging her to send someone to meet me. I knew there were no taxis in Paris, and I had been assured that Madame la Comtesse had a car which she used for her Red Cross work.

Imagine my consternation when one of my fellow-passengers casually complained that Gare St-Lazare would not be reopened until the next day, 1st June. The French in London had forgotten that I was travelling on 31st May.

The flat of my unknown hostess was situated miles from the Gare du Nord. No taxis. Only the one method of transport — the dreaded overcrowded Metro. I had too much hand-baggage to manage such a journey alone, and had no idea how far from the nearest Metro station my unknown hostess lived. I hoped that she would have realised the mistake and would be at the station — with car — to meet me.

I confided my anxieties to the naval officer, and at the same time asked him the size of tip the porter — if one could be found — would now expect. He told me that he would take charge of me and my baggage until we found my hostess, bless him. But not until we reached that seething terminus did it occur to me that never having met her before I was extremely unlikely to meet her now — even if she came in person and did not send a deputy — male or female. The brain fag of weeks must be my excuse for overlooking so important a detail.

My naval officer secured the ONLY porter, with a gigantic four-wheeled trolley on which he piled a mountain of American soldiers' baggage, with mine stuck like insignificant barnacles on the top, and we processed down the immense platform. At the barrier, among the hundreds of expectant faces I saw not one looking as though it expected me. I was asked by my escort *and* the porter, who was meeting me, and I was obliged idiotically to reply that I hadn't an idea. My poor naval officer could not linger in this uncertainty for longer than a quarter of an hour, and then, when no one claimed me, he was obliged to go off to keep an appointment with a superior officer. But before he went he paid the porter and confided me to his particular care.

Fortunately for me the porter was *un brave homme*. He suggested that when he had put the American luggage in the *Consigne Militaire* he should transfer mine to a hand barrow, and together we should tour the vast terminus until we found the mysterious person who might —

or might not — be there to meet me. This we did, he singing loudly a gay song of his own improvisation:

"Nous cherchons — nous ne savons pas qui
Peut-être c'est un Monsieur?
Peut-être c'est une Dame?
Allons-y";

which greatly refreshed my tired and anxious soul. At last, having toured that station twice, we trundled ourselves outside it and began to question the chauffeur of every stationary car. Did he come from the Comtesse de X? No, he never did. Finally, foot-sore, giddy with fatigue, I questioned the last of the line, a little man in a little private car. He, also, denied the Comtesse de X. Then my porter explained my predicament and asked if his car were for hire. No, it was not — but if Madame were *en panne* he could drive her to her destination — at a price.

Now it begins, I thought, feeling at that moment that no price would be too great to get to a bed, but remembering with anguish that I had only two thousand francs in my purse, and that I had been warned that to take a taxi anywhere in Paris cost over one thousand francs.

The little man looked at me (*did* he see the weariness in my eyes?), and asked me if I should consider one hundred francs too much? I nearly embraced him. I fell into that car, my luggage was piled in after me by my friendly porter, and we started to cross the dimly lit — but LIT — streets of Paris. The old sensation — something that grips the heart and takes away the breath — which has always seized me on entering Paris overwhelmed me now. The beautiful city, practically unharmed after all these years of war. I began to tell my companion of my joy to be back again — of my love for the Crillon, Notre-Dame, the Arc de Triomphe, and with a gleam in his eyes he took me to see one after another, a lovely little tour of Paris, before he finally deposited me at the haven where I would be. Then he leaped out of his car, opened the door, handed me and my baggage out, received his one hundred francs with a beautiful bow — and drove away.

And I had been told that I should find anti-English feeling in France; that I should fall among thieves. Thank God, I never really believed it. Always I have found both courtesy and kindness (and in the South something even more precious). This first journey proved me right.

The end of that day took on the quality of a strange and romantic dream. A Frenchwoman with a rather formidable face answered my ring. She looked me over suspiciously, but having weighed me in the balance, apparently did not find me wanting, for her hostile manner slowly began to dissolve as she led me into the dark hall and told me that she would inform Madame la Comtesse of my arrival.

Soon afterwards there appeared in a doorway the loveliest woman I have ever seen. Swathed in black draperies, her exquisite oval face startingly white in contrast to the winged dark hair swept back from perfectly chiselled features, so fine and transparent that it was difficult to believe that this was a woman of flesh and blood and not of a statue of Our Lady of Sorrows, she stood, framed in a dark doorway, her long white fragile hands outstretched in welcome, a smile lighting sad violet eyes under their pencilled brows.

So this was la Comtesse de X., one of the heroines of the Resistance, who, for hiding and saving the lives of so many of our fallen airmen, had suffered long imprisonment, untold miseries and unspeakable indignities, and who narrowly escaped death at the vile hands of the Germans.

This was my hostess, so thin, so ethereal, so exquisitely fragile, a tall wand of a woman but with a spirit of steel.

While I was regaining my breath she explained to me in a lovely low voice that she had sent her son to meet me at the Gare St-Lazare, as I had said. He would doubtless soon return, having failed to find me. She was so terribly sorry for the contretemps — I must be very tired. She ought to have realised that the trains would not change till to-morrow — *to-day* it is now, as she glanced at the clock. What could she do for me? Had I eaten? Would I like a hot drink? The English tea perhaps, she had a little, a gift from an English friend, but coffee France had not seen for a very long time. The beautiful courtesy and grace of old France.

There came a ring of the bell.

"That will be my son," she said, and opened the door to reveal a gigantic white-turbaned figure wearing a glorious rose-red cloak, who clicked his heels and bowed as his blue eyes twinkled at me from a sun-browned face.

I shall never, NEVER get over the fact that I missed

being met at the station by a wonderful officer of the Spahis. Incredible, almost, that this blond giant could be the son of that lovely wraith of a woman.

Then I was shown to my room with its soft longed-for French bed. So ended a day and a half.

CHAPTER
FIVE

Paris and the R.A.F.

I was thankful for the consideration for hungry countries shown by the British authorities, for with the 15 lbs. of food allowed for a month's visit I could be independent of the generosity of my hostess, except for a little bread for breakfast, and even that was strictly rationed. In return I could give her the longed-for luxury of *real* coffee. To enable her household to live, the Comtesse was obliged to travel into the country, always in that terrible Metro (for, long ago, her car had been given up), to fetch vegetables from the garden of her château, and anything else she could find, returning with her heavy baskets, faint with fatigue and the vitiated atmosphere of that horrible underground train.

I learned, in only two days, to hate and dread the battle of the Metro. One Frenchwoman told me that as she boarded a train during "the rush hour" all the windows, the whole length of the train, cracked and fell out on to the line from the pressure of bodies within. I could well believe it, having travelled with a very fat Frenchman affixed to my back like a plaster, and wearing a large American private soldier as a chest protector. He quietly chewed peppermint gum in my face, and, as he skilfully rolled it from side to side of a gaping mouth, I could almost see his tonsils. I could make no movement of any sort, and was eventually spewed forth from that train — I can't remember where, but not at the station for which I had booked — by the volition of the mass of humanity behind me. The *chic* Parisians had bicycles, and it was a common sight to see monsieur or madame, when on a shopping expedition, pedalling energetically through the streets with their purchases packed into a wooden store-box on wheels attached to the rear of the bicycle.

The sounds of Paris had changed. No longer the high-powered purr and deep-noted klaxon of the powerful private cars nor the pip-squeak horns of innumerable taxis. Instead, the roar of American lorries and jeeps, and, in the quiet streets, the clop-clop-clop of wooden-soled shoes. In the early mornings, before the military traffic began, Paris might have been one of the mill towns of the North of England with sabots clacking over cobblestones. For there was no leather left in France, and the shortage of footwear was one of the worst the French had to bear. In Paris it broke my heart to hear the limping children. One little girl, walking with her mother in front of me, kept stumbling and whimpering. I asked her mother what ailed the child, and for reply she lifted the foot of her child to show me burst and outgrown shoes, the heel under the blistered instep.

"They grow so fast, the children, madame, and when their shoes are too small, still they must wear them. Each child has one *bon* (coupon) for one pair of shoes a year.

24

But the shoes do not exist, or, if one should find a pair, it will be of the wrong size or else at a price impossible for the poor."

I went up to Montmartre and watched some children playing on a sand-heap in a smutty public garden. Pale, emaciated, knock-kneed little things, most of them rickety, all victims of malnutrition; the elder children with ugly decayed teeth — no calcium. Pathetic beyond words.

I have nightmare remembrances of that visit to Paris. It was very hot, and I hate great heat. It was necessary to visit Ministries, and no lifts were working because of the shortage of electricity. It was necessary to climb marble stairways to the fourth or fifth floor; one's papers were never ready, and one was asked to call again in an hour's time. That staircase must be descended and then climbed again, and, in the meantime, where and how to pass the intervening hour? In old days it would have been easy to sit on a chair outside a café, drink iced lemonade and watch the passers-by, but the only desperate occasion when I entered a teashop and asked for a tiny water-ice (three mouthfuls) the bill for forty francs turned me dizzy. I handed a fifty-franc note to the waitress, and she gave me a Metro ticket for change. I informed her that I was in uniform and treated *"En Militaire"* so did not pay for Metro tickets.

"Eh bien; c'est pour le service," said the maiden perkily, and shot my fifty-franc note into a drawer. I decided then that I would starve rather than spend such sums upon my suffering body, and, for the first day, I nearly did. I had been told to go for my meals to the

Y.W.C.A. canteen, which was superbly organised and very cheap, but no one had given me its address — and *you* try to explain Y.W.C.A. to a Parisian!

If I had been told that it was in *l'ancienne Maison Rumpelmeyer*, Rue Faubourg-St-Honoré, all would have been easy, but I walked for miles, sweating in my heavy uniform, in search of that place, until I accosted a red-tabbed English officer who directed me to it at once. Inside I found perfect peace and comfort; little tables laid with spotless cloths and cutlery; flowers, superb lighting, swift service and smiling faces, and OH! what food. American rations and a French chef with Gallic imagination and resource. Three courses, of which meat was always one, and good coffee for luncheon, at a cost of 24 francs. In the Café de Paris one could pay 500 or 600 francs for a meal not half as good, and it was really pathetic to see the number of hungry French who strove to be admitted to this place of peace and plenty. Some, in uniform, got in. (The franc was then only 176 to the £.)

Upstairs luxurious armchairs, writing-tables, English and American newspapers, free telephone, a service of interpreters and guides, and a glorious tea (and coffee), with brioches or buns toasted and oozing real butter and luscious cakes, for only 8 francs.

When I asked one of the English officials how it was done, she replied, "American food. But we shall be out of pocket on the service side; we must employ the French, and that man who bows you into your chair gets eight thousand francs a month for doing just that, and the girls who polish the spoons get three thousand francs a month.

Whereas *our* girls, with English pay, can just afford an occasional haircut, but *not* a shampoo as well."

My greatest shock came when I visited Cook's Travel Bureau near the Madeleine and asked the price of a ticket to the South. I was told that *single* fare second class, without a wagon-lit, would cost me 1,400 francs to Cannes, so that a return ticket would cost 2,800 and I had only the permitted 2,000 francs — slightly diminished by the cost of living in Paris — and I had to go on living in France for a month.

It was in this moment of panic when only God could get me out of the hole I was in, that HE did. You know that silent moment of panic when your brain whizzes round like the wheels of a car on wet grass, spinning madly but getting you nowhere? Well — I just let my brain spin for a little space of stricken silence, and then into that silence a voice whispered:

"Ring up that wonderful Resistance man you met in London, Commandant M. He gave you his number and promised his help should you need it."

The perverse woman in me argued:

"But he's half the time in London, and surely will be there now."

"Ring him up," repeated the voice.

So I rang him up. And he was there. At once he invited me to dine with his wife and himself, and I spent a lovely evening with them in their top-floor flat, all light and air. I poured forth all my troubles, and in five minutes the problem of transport was solved. An appointment was made for me, by telephone, to see our Air Attaché at the English Embassy next day. Since I was being sent on a "special mission" by the French, I was handed over to the R.A.F., and with their adoption of me began a new phase of my adventure.

I was collected next day by a soldier in a jeep. He threw my baggage into it, helped me into the seat beside him, and then drove at a terrifying speed to the office of the R.A.F. in the Place Vendôme. That drive was, to say the least of it, an exhilarating experience, and I am thankful to say that though several French citizens narrowly escaped with their lives we didn't kill anyone. But at that time the English and American armies had practically taken possession of Paris, and pedestrians lived with their eyes on stalks.

At the office of the R.A.F. I was received with such kindness that my lonely apprehensions began to fade.

After handing in my papers and being weighed with my baggage, which formality took exactly three minutes, I was led to a luxurious armchair and served with hot coffee and brioches. At last I could relax: I was being taken care of, and all I had to do until I reached the South of France was to submit to this delicious sensation.

"Cigarette with your coffee, Lady Fortescue? Your car will be here in twenty minutes to take you to Le Bourget."

My car! What music in those two words to one who had fought the battle of the Metro for five weary days. I leant back, and enjoyed my coffee and cigarette until ushered forth to take my place in the first of a fleet of lovely cars into which various important personages stepped, while W.A.A.F.s and airmen climbed into a private auto-bus.

Then the procession, led by insignificant ME, roared on its way to the aerodrome of Le Bourget.

I had never flown in my life. Indeed, when flying first began I had voiced a rash vow that I would never fly. How a situation — and a war — can change our ideas! Here was I, rescued from a difficult predicament by the R.A.F. and only too thankful to be strapped into a bomber with the prospect of reaching my destination swiftly, and avoiding the discomfort of spending perhaps two or three days on an overcrowded train with no restaurant car.

I was the only woman in the plane with several officers of the R.A.F. From their demeanour and that of the pilot, who handed "the stick" over to a friend while he came to see that I was comfortable, one might almost have thought that this was my own private bomber. Was I cold? Someone produced a rug. Did I find the scooped iron seat too hard? Indeed I *did*, and then someone, kindly considering my latter end, inflated two life-saving jackets, one to be used as a seat and one to comfort my unsupported back. My neighbour offered me a bar of chocolate, which I felt it wiser to refuse having heard of air-sickness. Another boy handed me a novel to read, but this I also refused, being far too interested in watching over my shoulder under the wing of the plane the landscape below me becoming ever more and more like a tiny flat map as we flew to higher altitudes. Sitting sideways in a plane instead of facing the way one is going is not conducive to sightseeing, and after a time gives a crick in the neck if one persists in peering outwards. My companions had evidently long since realised this, for they fell into a gentle doze or read novels, though one or other of them did point out some neat bit of bombing previously achieved. The president of my fund, dear General Sicé, had adjured me to study during the flight the French rivers all the way from Paris to Marseilles, telling me that I should then get some idea of their difficulties of transport. So I continued to crick my neck, and as we flew onwards, always I saw the silver ribbons which were rivers unbroken by any bridge. Only one temporary bridge did I see on that journey; all the rest had been destroyed. How many years would it take poor France to recover from this ghastly devastation?

We reached the Alpes Maritimes, and here the air pockets caused the bomber to dance and plunge a bit, but triumph of triumphs I did not become air-sick. Rolling a fearful eye at the neat row of paper bags suspended within reach above us, I felt that I should never again be able to hold up my head if compelled to use one of those humiliating contrivances. On our return journey, three weeks later, they were torn down and filled with peaches bought from barrows in Marseille by joyous South African pilots on their way to visit relatives in the Mother Country and anxious to arrive laden with gifts.

When we reached the airport of Marseille and stiffly descended from the plane, the pilot came up to me and asked me how I had enjoyed my first flight. "Very much — but we didn't go very fast," I commented, "and the wing of the plane blocked my view badly." He twinkled at me.

"Well, we never flew at a less speed than two hundred miles per hour," he retorted, "and unluckily I couldn't very well alter the construction of the plane."

Impossible to realise how fast we were flying, for at that great height the landscape below seemed stationary for long periods of time.

I had been promised in Paris that a car should deliver me to my door, and now I was invited to refresh myself in the canteen while transport of some sort was secured for me. But it so happened that the R.A.F. cars were all away on long-distance journeys, and the French Red Cross car also was out on a mission.

"If you don't mind staying for the night a car will be at your disposal to-morrow morning," said the Wing Commander. I gazed at him mutely and, I suppose, piteously.

"Only for one night," he strove to reassure me. "Much less tiring for you, really, for it's a pretty long way to your mountain village from here, and you've travelled a bit already. But of course I understand that you want to get quickly to your own place, and I'm terribly sorry there isn't an available car to-day."

"It isn't that — it's — you see," I stammered, "I'm scared stiff of French prices. You see, I was only allowed to bring out two thousand francs — there's a hole in it already, and a night in a Marseilles hotel will probably swallow it all up — and I've got to live somehow for three or four weeks. I couldn't even have got to the Midi if the R.A.F. hadn't adopted me —"

"But of course you are still in our care," he answered. "We ask you to be our guest of honour in the funny little hotel we've requisitioned. You'll forgive a soldier's camp bed and the simplicity of your room, I hope, and we'll try to make you as comfortable as possible."

Oh, angels of the air! . . .

Before I got into my camp bed I dined in the mess, and was afterwards taken to a little cinema next door which had been opened for the troops. In the courtyard at the back of the hotel there stood a gigantic magnolia in full bloom, and the exotic lemony scent of the flowers mingled with the equally exotic but less romantic smell of hot American negroes, who were doing queer jazz movements and shuffle dances to the strains of the mechanical music issuing from within the cinema. June in Provence can be very hot indeed, and *la grande chaleur* was just beginning. The atmosphere inside the cinema was indescribable as hot wafts of it rose to the gallery reserved for officers, where I was sitting. I was too dazed to analyse it closely, but I recognised a strong undercurrent of garlic, which made me realise, even in my waking-dreaming condition that I was — I really WAS — back again in my beloved Provence.

I hardly slept at all, but it wasn't the fault of that hard little bed. In only a few hours I should be home again after five years of exile. I should drive down the stony mountain track to the great door of Fort Escu, and I should clang the bell suspended from the wall to summon my faithful Margharita. How would she look? Ill and emaciated after all the privations she had suffered? Would she still be the inarticulate Margharita who could only express her feelings with those huge brown almond-shaped eyes, fringed around by phenomenal lashes, and by the twisting of her long thin fingers? Would she still look at her *Madame* with love in those clear eyes? And my little "Sunset House"?

My beloved garden? Then with a sick feeling I pictured the visit that must be made to Mademoiselle's château, entering its courtyard and seeing no little oval face peering through the curtain of corks which swung over the front entrance. In England, in hours of loneliness, I had so often pictured our rapturous re-union after these tragic years of separation, the ecstatic barking of the dogs, The Blackness careering madly round the courtyard and the secret garden, in chase of Squibs, having first nearly overpowered his adored *Mademoiselle* with his exuberant joy. And so I had found comfort. But now there would be no *Mademoiselle* and there was no Blackness — but there would still be little Squibs, her shadow dog. How should I find our peasant neighbours? Who would have survived this ghastly war? The hours of the night dragged slowly on, and the approaching day would answer many of the questions of my heart. From my bed I stared out of the uncurtained window at a magnolia blossom which swayed across it, magically lovely in the moonlight, and in the darkness before dawn I fell asleep and the pale ivory flower became the face of Elisabeth Starr.

CHAPTER
SIX

Return to "Sunset House"

Hardly had I finished a last cup of real American coffee next morning when an orderly announced that my car was at the door. Various officers came to see me off, and I was informed that the car was at my disposal for the whole day, so that if I wanted to go by the longer route, *via* Cannes, to get in touch with the French Red Cross officials and visit the English Bank, I could do this without fear of upsetting Army plans.

"I've given you rather a dour Scot as a driver, but what he lacks in conversational powers he makes up in knowledge of cars, so that if you should have a break-down of any sort he's competent to deal with it," said the Wing Commander, kind and careful for my welfare to the last.

"I can never thank the R.A.F. enough for all they have done for me personally," I said in farewell. "Our debt as a nation is already far beyond payment except by our pride in such a service, and our gratitude. How I wish the R.A.F. could instil some of its marvellous efficiency and organisation into poor chaotic France."

My dour Scot grunted as he put the car into gear and we drove away. Dust and glare, stony half-repaired

34

roads damaged by bombing, detours farther inland where bridges had been destroyed, then vineyards, a few parasol pines splintered by shell fire, glimpses of one of the bluest seas in the world, silvery olive trees clothing mountain slopes splashed with golden Spanish broom. So familiar, so infinitely dear. We approached Cannes and my chauffeur was obliged to stop to locate some strange noises in the engine unheard by me, and while he was peering under the bonnet a piteous old woman hobbled up to my window. She looked like the oldest woman in the world, so thin, so pale, so wrinkled, wrapped in incredible rags, a torn skirt displaying a twisted deformed and swollen leg, while burst shreds of rag tied on with string revealed bleeding, blistered feet. She begged me for the love of God to drive her the remaining miles to the Mairie for a relief ration of bread. She held up the deformed leg and foot, which looked as though they had been broken and badly mended.

"Ah, Madame, mes pieds me font mal," she wailed. When — if ever — she reached the Mairie she must stand for hours in a queue, and then walk home again. She could not hurry, and probably would have had the journey for nothing, for the bread very often was not enough to go round. The chauffeur looked up from his tinkering, met my imploring gaze, and shook his head vigorously.

"Oh, can't we take her as far as the Mairie?" I pleaded. "Look how old and tired she is! Look at her awful feet!"

"Army regulations," he answered shortly. "We're forbidden to pick up any civilians, and the Yanks are even more severe than we are, and they're occupying Cannes. It does seem hard when there's room in the car — but there are hundreds like her, and if we gave a lift to one! — You see, there's no buses, no trams or transport of any sort. I'm sorry, madam," as I began to plead again, "but this is an Army car, and I must obey orders or I shall get into serious trouble." Unanswerable. I tried to explain this to that pitiful old woman who stared beseechingly into my eyes, beating her breast and repeating, *"Pour l'amour de Dieu, Madame!"* while tears of misery and exhaustion poured down her face. And I could do nothing. As we drove away she cried after me weakly, *"Ah, vous n'êtes pas gentille, vous n'êtes pas gentille!"* If she could only have known the pain it was to me to leave her thus. The vision of her haunts me still. That was the beginning. Every day I must witness misery such as that: prisoners of war returning wrecked in health from concentration camps, children with tuberculosis, rickets and skin diseases from malnutrition. I had come out to make a report, and I must see these terrible things; for only thus could I convince others that the need of France was desperate. She must and should be helped in her distress.

We drove to the English Bank, where before the war I had rented a small safe in which to keep a few precious things — Mummie's letter to me written on my first birthday, her Bible, and some letters from my man. Before leaving France, while I was frantically packing up John's books, the silver, the old glass and so on, I had asked *Mademoiselle* to collect my treasures from the Bank as she was going to Cannes. I gave her the key of my safe and a letter of authorisation, but when she returned in the evening she told me sadly that French law insisted that the contents of private safes be given only to the owner, who must sign many forms before being allowed to take anything away. I left early next morning, so was obliged to leave my treasures behind, and now I expected to be told that when the Germans occupied Cannes they had looted all banks and rifled the safes. Finding only things of no value to them in mine they would surely have thrown them out as rubbish. But no! The bank manager assured me that my safe was intact, and in it I found all I sought, blue with mildew — but THERE. Psychic people have always assured me that I am "protected," and this was the third instance of the protection of my property in France. My little "Sunset House" and my faithful *bonne* inside it both safe and untouched. John's books and pictures, our glass and silver, which I had transferred to a friend's house in Grasse when an Englishwoman occupied my house on my departure, also intact. And now, down in Cannes, my precious personal papers also safe; it seemed and seems to me miraculous. Hugging my mouldy little packet, I drove to the small hotel reserved for the R.A.F., where I had yet another example of their chivalry and hospitality. Both my driver and I were given an excellent luncheon, and after an interval of rest, for the heat at midday was intense, we set forth again and started our climb up to Opio.

At Valbonne the bridge had been blown up, and we had to descend a steep and narrow track on the edge of the crater, but the road through the pine-woods beyond was exactly the same. We roared through the village of Opio, climbing the last hill, but no one knew of my coming, and I saw no familiar figures about — only a few children, babies when I left and strange to me now, who shouted with excitement at the phenomenon of a passing car. The little signpost with FORT ESCU painted upon it and an arrow pointing down the mountain track which led to my house was actually still there and standing upright. How many times in 1939 had it been knocked down or biffed askew by the lorries of French soldiers! but someone had replaced it, and this time planted it in a pudding of cement for security. We turned the hairpin bend, and there stood my little Fort dreaming in the hot sunshine. The great wall surrounding it was completely covered by a wild riot of climbing roses and honeysuckle which, planted inside it, had run madly up and over it, and were now trailing across the stony neglected road. The cypresses I had grown from seed in the other *domaine* towered above the wall. What should I find inside? With a heavily beating heart I pulled the rusty chain of the bell suspended by the great door and then — waited. Absolute silence. I rang again more loudly, and then I heard swift padding footsteps shuffling across the courtyard, the inner bars and bolts were shot back, the great door opened — and there stood my Margharita! Thin as a rail, browned by the sun, for she had been gallantly doing the work of a man since the liberation, tilling the ground, tending the vines and olive trees. I had left her slim and smart, wearing a pale lemon-coloured dress, her mop of curly brown hair bound by a scarlet silk handkerchief and her feet shod in scarlet sandals. Now she was nearly in rags;

a torn overall covered her gaunt limbs, her buzz of hair unruly, and her feet — oh! her feet. . . . Burst sand-shoes with soles flapping loose revealed her long brown toes. Her high cheek-bones seemed trying to come through the stretched skin of her face; her eyes, always large, were now enormous, and when she saw me standing there they seemed to fill her face.

"Madame! Ah, Madame! Ma Madame!" was all that she could say as she flung herself into my outstretched arms and sank her head, quietly sobbing great deep sobs upon my shoulder. For once we changed places; the flood-gates were opened; and after years of loneliness, she, the inarticulate Margharita, inundated me with speech, bombarding me with questions about my health, how had I come, when did I first set foot in France, how were all my family, and England — poor England — while I, the more voluble, could say nothing at all, only stroke her curls and look into those faithful spaniel's eyes, so like my Dominie's now in their expression of utter love and trust.

And Dominie, her *"Petit Noir"?* . . . At length she led me into the courtyard, and I stared about me at the mad luxuriance of all that I had planted. Margharita had only been able to work the vegetable garden to keep herself alive. She had watered the roses and plants and creepers of Madame, but could not prune them or control their wild growth. No wire in France, no nails — the only ladder rotted away. I felt like Rip Van Winkle or the Sleeping Beauty, awaking from their dreams to find themselves in the same place rendered unfamiliar by the passage of years. The *persiennes* (shutters) of my house could no longer be closed because of the great sprays of bignonia and stentonia which had rushed up the walls and claimed the house as their own. To enter the loggia I had to push my way through a tangle of climbing geraniums, and the little Paulownia tree given me by *Mademoiselle*, which reached only to my shoulder when I left, was now trying to push over the house, and blocked the view from the highest windows. Colour and scent and a mad extravagance of growth everywhere. I was even glad to enter the cool, dark hall-dining-room, now shaded from the sun, to rest my eyes from the blaze of light and colour and my tired soul from an excess of emotion.

But I was not allowed to rest. I must make a tour of my little home while Margharita gave an account of her stewardship. She had tried to protect *les belles choses de Madame*, but with cleaning materials so impossible to get it had been difficult. Still, she had hoarded supplies that I had left and used them very sparingly. I could never have believed it possible to find, after six years of war and enemy occupation, so perfect an interior. My little "Sunset House" looked as smart and new as when I had first occupied it. Brasses winked in dark corners; in my studio upstairs the white curtains and covers were spotless; the grey-tiled floors were clean and polished. In my bedroom the azalea-tinted curtains also had been washed, and the sinking sun glowing through them cast a warm reflection on the silver-painted wood surrounding my divan bed. It was almost too wonderful to be believed, and what it represented almost too poignant to be borne. I had thought my little home lost for ever — it might be a ruined heap of stones, destroyed by a bomb; or looted and desecrated by enemy occupation — and I found it perfect.

"Oh Margharita! Ma chère, ma fidèle Margharita!" was all that I could say. *"Comment vous remercier?"* How could I ever express to her my gratitude for such fidelity and loving service during my long absence?

"C'était pour ma Madame," said Margharita simply, grown inarticulate again, and her Madame humbly realised how unworthy she was of such devotion.

Last we visited my little kitchen. The yellow-tiled floor was as clean as ever, but a hideous object in the middle drew from me an exclamation. Margharita hastily explained that since there was no fuel in the South of France she had been obliged to use the little stove which once our washerwoman employed to boil water. Only a few sticks were necessary to make a fire with this tiny round stove, and she had fixed its rusty iron chimney into that of the kitchener, naturally at a drunken angle. Collecting dead twigs from the olive trees, using only a saucepan or a frying-pan, because of course there was no oven, and doing her work either on her knees or in a squatting position, so had poor Margharita cooked for herself during these last years. I looked at my splendid little kitchener, which once also heated water for luxurious hot baths until coal and its substitutes became extinct; then at my Butagaz stove, which had been used in hot weather like this until all supplies of gas failed, and finally at the electric rings, kettle and toaster, which had been such joys to us in the early mornings until all electricity had been cut off. *Mademoiselle*, my architect, had thought out every possibility of avoiding domestic annoyances for me. If the coal merchant failed to deliver our fuel, then there would be the Butagaz in reserve. If the gas-cylinder died on me before its substitute arrived there would always be electricity to help me out. What neither of us foresaw was the awful possibility of enemy occupation in the land of our ally, who, we thought, had one of the strongest armies in the world; and that my poor Margharita would be obliged to erect this Heath Robinson contraption in one of the most modern and convenient little kitchens in Provence in order to cook her scanty food. It was still very scanty. She prepared a banquet for me that night: a minute cup of vegetable soup (three years of drought and the cutting off of the water supply had been fatal for every one's vegetables) and some haricot beans *sauté* in a few drops of rare and precious olive oil (rare because the Germans, not content with the theft of nearly all the olive oil of Provence, had mined some of the olive groves on their departure so that the peasants could neither tend and prune their olive trees nor gather the crop). I had not yet my food card, so Margharita spared me a slice of her meagre ration of dark bread, which when toasted became darker still, and for dessert I ate one of my own scarce peaches, scarce again owing to the drought and the lack of spraying materials to kill parasites and prevent *la maladie*. Pests had multiplied in a terrifying manner, because every bird, cat or dog (except a few *chiens de chasse* to hunt non-existent rabbits and partridges) had been shot and eaten during the worst period of hunger in 1943.

While Margharita was on her knees in the kitchen preparing the banquet I was on mine in my little chapel built in the rocks, saying prayers of thankfulness that my home had been spared and she within it, and for all the happy past years spent in this lovely land surrounded by such love. Almost I saw the slender hands of *Mademoiselle* hanging the bronze figure of the Christ, which she found buried in the mud of Flanders during the war of 1914-18, above the little font. Sunset light flooded the chapel from the window of the rugged cloister, staining the great boulders under the primitive arch where stood the altar with a blood-red radiance against which the black shadow of the beautiful carved cross behind it stood out in bold relief. Thank God no more blood was being shed! The Cross had triumphed, but even so, the world had been crucified, as *Mademoiselle* had said it would be. The victims of this war were numbered in millions. I prayed for strength and courage to help bind up some of those war wounds in this my chosen corner, a lone crusader now.

I came out into the sunset. At such an hour ten years ago I had found the little ruinous cottage of stone dreaming in the sunset glow, and had softly quoted to myself the doggerel verse beginning:—

"Little sunset house of hearts
Standing all alone. . . ."

I had loved it at sight and wanted it. To-day it was still mine, transformed by the genius of *Mademoiselle* into a perfect little dwelling place in the loveliest corner of

43

Provence. No modern building disfigured it; only old stone houses, marked by their sentinel cypresses "Peace" and "Prosperity," nestled amid the olive groves that clothed the slopes of those rounded hills. The little olive mill stood with its wheel and tiny viaduct; and perched on mountain peaks was the tiny village of Opio, with its square Mairie, the church with the thirteenth-century clock tower and an ancient *Mas* or two, dominated on a higher peak by the little town of dreams and deep sweet bells, Châteauneuf-de-Grasse, the most exquisite of all the little mountain towns.

It was the magic moment of the red ray when every flower becomes a glowing translucent jewel. I looked down into my garden of English roses. Perforce they had been neglected, some of the trees were dead, and briars thrived among the lovelier blossoms; they needed pruning and cultivation by loving hands. But the red ray transformed each flower into a fairy lamp with an effect so wonderful that defects became invisible. I lifted my eyes to the hills already becoming mysterious with the blue mists of evening. The sun sank behind the distant mountains, and among the olive groves there were deep violet shadows. Cypresses on the skyline showed black against the afterglow, and a golden sickle of a moon shone low with its brilliant attendant star against a sky of clear Nile green. During that long hot drive home I had pestered God with a small but urgent request (as if He hadn't enough to do without being badgered for so insignificant a thing).

"Oh, please let me be greeted by at least *one* firefly on my first night; I shall feel so much less lonely."

I was so afraid that our fireflies might have come — and gone. And there was the answer to my prayer, flickering towards me through the dim olive grove from *Mademoiselle*'s château as though her radiant spirit had come to comfort me. Only God could remember so humble a request. Only He could pay such attention to detail.

CHAPTER
SEVEN

Mademoiselle's Little Hospital

The next day I needed all the courage for which I had prayed. I must go down to *Mademoiselle*'s château to visit the courageous woman whom she had sheltered during the war, and who, thank God, was there to nurse her with a matchless devotion when she fell ill. How should I be able to bear to enter that courtyard and find no Elisabeth? But there would be little Squibs, who would give me the same rapturous greeting, for dogs NEVER forget those they once have loved.

But not even Squibs ran to welcome me. Only three days before my arrival she had gently fallen asleep in her basket, and was now certainly romping joyously with *Mademoiselle* in the Elysian fields.

And the heartbreak that I had expected to feel as I approached those loved haunts I did not feel. It was as though Elisabeth ran to meet me and led me into the home we both loved so much, with our rampageous dogs at our heels. . . .

The rest of that day was one long series of embraces. Never in my life have I been so frequently or so fervently kissed by peasants, both male and female. My face salted by their tears and my skin pricked by the bristles of many beards, for my home-coming was at the end of a week, and no man is shaved in Provence except on Saturday night or Sunday morning. The bristles were unusually profuse and strong owing to the tropical heat. They all told me that to them I was like a "second landing" — the first Englishwoman to come back after these years of anguish. I was told pitiful tales of hardship and hunger, illustrated by expressive gestures, the most frequent the tightening of the belt until no vacant holes were left. They had lived on dandelions and animal turnips, had made soup from grass, coffee from acorns, tobacco from — well — any weed.

I missed familiar faces, victims of hardship like their beloved *Mademoiselle*. Only the news from London — *"Ici Londres"* — relayed from the B.B.C., and listened to hungrily in secret by all who possessed hidden crystal sets, and the heartening of *Mademoiselle*, who received them at night in her château, explained the progress of the Allies, and always before parting made them drink the toast. *"A la Victoire"* had kept up their morale in those dark days. Even during periods of discouragement her confidence in ultimate victory was never shaken. Always that gay toast, *"A la Victoire,"* drunk in the good wine of her vineyards; always the V-sign when she met her peasant neighbours. So that on her grave had been planted a gigantic V in white English pinks from my garden and that sacred place bordered with old grey stones from her own mountain.

Of all people in the world *Mademoiselle* should have

been here to greet the liberating army. She who had never faltered in her faith should have been alive to see victory. So they mourned. I had known that I should find their grief echoing mine, hardest of all to bear.

The next day I started to fulfil my mission. The telephone service was still dreadful and depleted. A call to Grasse took from two to three hours to get through instead of one minute. The weariness and often the frustration of attempting to contact mayors, doctors and other officials was a great strain, but eventually I did succeed in making a few appointments. Fortunately the Mayor of Grasse had a small supply of petrol; and since I had come out by his invitation, and he had the health of the children of this region very deeply at heart, he put the mayoral car at my disposal and constituted himself as my chauffeur.

In the broiling sunshine he, his *Adjoint* and sometimes his wife collected me daily, and we visited every tottering *oeuvre* and every empty house which might perhaps be bought to form the nucleus of the permanent relief centre of my dreams. It was depressing work, because every existing crèche, orphanage, hospital or dispensary was in such dire need of — EVERYTHING. Sheets mended and patched had fallen into rags, blankets had been used until they were bald, or had been corrupted by moth (for every pest-destroyer had long ago become extinct); and there were now no needles with which to darn; no mending wool; no soap to wash people or clothes, only a sandy substitute they called *"ciment."* Clotted wool was bursting from mattresses, windows gaped without panes, for glass was unobtainable; the hospitals lacked bandages, gauze, rubber sheets, instruments, and even found it difficult to feed their patients, for so much crockery had been broken and could not be replaced. Every one lacked food, even the country peasants who had been obliged to kill their hens and their cows because, after the drought, there was no corn or pasture with which to feed them. The same story everywhere, the same decay and destitution. One thought encouraged me as I took note of all this misery; the clothes and comforts that through the marvellous generosity of readers of my books, and the children and teachers of so many schools and convents in England, I had collected and packed, would seem in this depleted and impoverished land a gift from heaven itself. That collection had seemed to be pitifully small and inadequate for the enormous needs of Provence, but now I saw that those eight thousand garments, those three hundred pairs of real leather shoes, those cots and blankets and medical stores would be of priceless value.

In Paris my dear General Sicé had been strongly against my returning to Provence before the winter, which he feared might prove too hard for me to bear.

"Wait until conditions improve," he pleaded.

"What is the meaning of the word RELIEF?" was my reply, and he looked at me with such a beautiful expression in his Breton blue eyes, patted my shoulder, and simply said, *"Que Dieu vous bénisse et vous garde,"* for of course my question could have but one answer, and he knew that I meant to go.

Everything that I saw now confirmed me in my resolve

to return quickly to England, see to the export of my one hundred and eight cases, and come back here as soon as possible. Prices were fantastic, and the lack of material to repair empty houses made it impossible at the moment to buy property or to build. But at least I could distribute the gifts and alleviate a little of this misery, and some of my fund (only about £5,000 in all, and there would be the costs of transport and of much printing to pay out of it) could be spent in repairing Elisabeth's little hospital of St. Christophe (for children suffering from *maladies osseuses*). It stands in an olive grove not far from my house, and I found it in piteous condition; for the roots of cypress trees had cracked the main drains, and an unsuspected sub-soil of clay had gaped and sunk under the hospital itself, causing sinkage and dangerous cracks in walls and ceilings. *Mademoiselle* had created it with such money as she and her friends could collect after the first Great War, and during this one all minor repairs had become impossible, and had developed into major injuries. The English directresses, who had nursed in France with *Mademoiselle* in the 1914 war, and had given their devoted voluntary service to the children of St. Christophe since 1928, had been obliged to rush back to England or be shut up in a concentration camp, but the French committee had gallantly kept the little hospital open under the direction of a Frenchwoman, aided only by a young girl with a tuberculous hip and a peasant who came for an hour or two to cook.

After my visit to St. Christophe it came to me that I must try to make *Mademoiselle*'s little hospital the nucleus of the permanent relief centre, my French

Chailey, gradually buy the surrounding land, build additional wings, perhaps a small operating-theatre with an X-ray department, and workshops to teach these disabled children trades, so making these pathetic little victims of the war (some of them maimed by allied bombing) useful citizens in spite of their disabilities. Dreams — dreams — with present prices my fund could hardly do more than pay for the repairs and perhaps the maintenance of the hospital for one year. But then I remembered the miracle wrought at Chailey. As a young wife and mother Mrs. Kimmins started with a five-pound note, a house condemned by the authorities as unfit for habitation, and seven cripples. From that beginning the prosperous colony of Chailey developed, with its four hundred joyous cripples all learning trades in lovely surroundings. She has a secret box in which written

DREAMS

— plans for enlargement of the exquisite chapel, for a large operating-theatre — and the remaining dreams will almost certainly come true as did the first, for a strong faith and a deep love can accomplish anything and everything.

Now I was dreaming too, but as yet I had no box. My dreams were kept inside my heart.

CHAPTER
EIGHT

Return is Difficult

To reach the South of France had been hard enough; to get away from it seemed to present insuperable difficulties. Foolishly I had imagined that when I had made all my visits, enquiries and notes I had only to telephone to the R.A.F. in Marseille, and they would collect me with one of their cars and fly me home. But I was now told that to get a telephone call through to Marseille was utterly impossible. Only the American and British armies could get long-distance calls put through after long hours of waiting, and when — or if — they succeeded, the voice at the other end of the wire was so faint and indistinct that it could seldom be understood. Very well, then, I would write. I was informed that letters usually took about three weeks to go across country and my *permis de séjour* expired in a week's time.

Standing in my rose garden that morning I could hear no sound of traffic. Utter silence — save when the clocks of Opio and Châteauneuf struck the hour, the one after the other, as though the Opio bell wanted to make sure that every one had heard the bell of Châteauneuf tell the time. It was like living in a lonely silent prison cut off from all the world. Very restful for residents, but I had to get back to England — somehow. In old days we had our cars, taxis could be hired from Grasse, motor buses ran regularly. Now — NOTHING. My one hope was a *camion*, for builders could get a small supply of petrol and there might be a lorry going to Marseille to fetch material. Failing this I must somehow get to Cagnes from whence the little spuffle-train left daily, full of soldiers, at 5 a.m. But how to get to Cagnes, many, many kilometres away?

It was then that the bell over the gateway suddenly clanged. I ran to it and drew back the heavy bolts to admit a very old friend, an *entrepreneur* of Magagnosc, who had not only repaired all our houses in the past, but had solved all our other problems as well with an exuberant kindness rarely to be found. He had always twinkled at us in our misfortunes and always laughingly set them right, even if he worked all day and all night to do it. During the war *Mademoiselle* had written to me and said, "Felicien is my very best friend," and this had not surprised me, for he had been the best friend of us all for so long.

Behold him now smiling widely and displaying a golden tooth, his kind brown eyes dancing with delighted anticipation of my pleasure when I should open the tiny parcel he handed me. Inside it was a toy *gigot* shorn from some starved little sheep. He had travelled up into the high mountains to persuade a friend to kill one of his precious sheep and spare one of its legs for *Madame*, since, coming from England where people were better fed, she would be suffering from hunger. She had been — she was — and this skinny little limb, which could not possibly supply more than one scanty meal for two people, was indeed a precious gift, rendered more so by the thoughtfulness and affection of the giver, who had lost a whole day's work to get it. Margharita actually paled with emotion when she saw it, and when she went down on her knees before Heath Robinson to cook it there was reverence in her attitude.

Felicien, of course, solved my transport problem. A spare part was needed for his *camion*; his partner wanted to get a parcel of eggs to Marseille, whence a relation, who was leaving for the north next week, could convey it to his hungry family. The journey to Marseille should be made on a day convenient to me, and I could go in his little car. Oh, blessed Felicien!

Gloom settled upon my Margharita when that day was fixed. Her eyelids drooped, her movements were listless, and she showed signs of animation only when feeding the three beloved hens she had acquired during my absence: one given to her by *Mademoiselle*, one given in exchange for a bottle of wine which she herself had made in the *lavoir* with a borrowed hand-press; and the third brought back from Italy under her arm when she returned from a holiday in Piedmont. Then she would cry, *"Poulie, Poulie, Poulie,"* while the half-starved birds fluttered all over her and her sad face relaxed into a smile. She had so hoped that now that *Madame* had come back she would never again leave home; and when I promised faithfully to return in the autumn, she only shook her head doubtingly, with a rather wry smile, and said, of course life must be far less hard in England, and why should *Madame* leave it to endure privations in

France? It was only good sense to stay where you were safe and comfortable. I understood it all so well. When we are very miserable there is a horrible urge in us all to lash out and hurt somebody — very often the person we love best. Why? I have never analysed though I have experienced that feeling.

On my last day Margharita was practically invisible. No answer when I called her in the house. No answer when I yelled in the garden. Perhaps she was in the vegetable garden outside the great gates. But she was nowhere until noon, when I suddenly heard her moving about in the kitchen. The same absences were repeated all through the day, and not until evening was the mystery of her disappearances explained, for I am not curious and had asked no questions. I was having dinner, served by Margharita, when the squeaky voice of one of the village children was heard calling her name. She flushed, hastily put down the dish she was offering to me, and rushed to the door. I heard whispering and wondered if this were yet another bouquet from the children of Opio — they had brought me so many, and one in particular of wild oats with their graceful oval bobbles painted red, white and blue as a compliment to England. But this time Margharita re-entered alone carrying — an enormous cake she had made for my journey. Having no fuel, she had taken it to the village baker to cook in his oven. All day long she had been running up and down our steep little mountain visiting the bakery to see if the cake was baked or *when* it would be baked, and how it was baking. She had hoarded some white flour from pre-war days for my return, she had used the eggs from her precious hens and flavoured the cake with a tiny tot of rum left her by my tenant in case of illness. These treasures she had kept FOR ME while starving herself. . . . You will all know how I felt. . . . If there is a flavour I dislike it is that of rum — a tragedy — but I could still appreciate the sacrifices that Margharita had made for her *Madame,* so I clasped the huge cake to a full heart, and she will never know. . . .

Farewells should be described briefly, and this time I left a hope of my return, laden with the things they lacked, to help my friends through the winter. None of them seemed quite able to believe that I should be able to keep my promise, but I felt that at least I had kindled a spark of hope in their anxious hearts.

We drove to Marseille by a route through the Var, chosen by my driver that I might see the place where the liberating allied army of the air descended in gliders and with parachutes. The roads and boundaries were still lined by hundreds of wrecked gliders, pulled out from among the vines by peasants who had since denuded them of anything that might be useful. They lay there, line upon line, looking like skeletons of gigantic prehistoric birds, and every woman or girl wore a head-band, sash or scarf of bright hued silk, made from those glorious parachutes, which looked very incongruous worn with pitifully ragged attire. What would I not have given to have seen that wonderful air-borne invasion of multi-coloured parachutes falling like flowers from this clear blue Mediterranean sky, and to have made one of the welcoming party on those sandy beaches *Mademoiselle* and I knew and loved so well!

At Marseille we were confronted by an unexpected and ridiculous difficulty. I had been told by the Wing Commander that if I were unable to telephone him the day I wished to go home, I must just arrive the previous day, stay the night in their hotel as before, and he would try to fix up a passage for me next morning. We had arrived late in the day, and I had been too weary to take note of landmarks, nor had I even asked the name of the modest hotel requisitioned by the R.A.F. I only knew that it was in a quiet little square surrounded by trees. The roaring traffic of Marseille, its wide crowded streets were now entirely unfamiliar and most bewildering, but in perfect confidence that every Marseillais would know where was situated the hotel of our famous (and so much beloved in France) R.A.F. I wasn't worrying at all. But no one had the vaguest idea where it was. My companion enquired of *gendarmes*, of soldiers, of civilians, of shopkeepers — but every one denied all knowledge of it, and he became irritable with anxiety because his supply of petrol had nearly run out and I had assured him that in Marseille it would be replenished by the R.A.F. The heat was almost unbearable, the flies maddening, and he was tired after the long drive, and anxious to rest and eat with his family.

"Drive to the first Union Jack," I said succinctly (in French). Surely a building decorated with our English flag could give me some information. He obeyed, and I toiled up three flights of stairs, entered an office, and was greeted with:

"Say, ma'am, yew look mighty warm. What can Amurrica do fer yew?"

"Why are you masquerading as English?" I asked him sweetly. "I'm English, and I want information, so I followed *our* flag."

"Wal, English and Amurrica can be said to be almost one and the same thing," he answered amiably, "an' we'll sure be glad to help yew ef we can. We've just borrowed your flag for the time bein'. The French seem to like the look of it."

Nice, generous boy. This was heart-warming — although he had never heard of an hotel occupied by the R.A.F. in Marseille.

"But — say, ma'am, yew're in luck, fer their 'boorow' fer transport is in the next street, an' they'll sure know about their H.Q."

We drove to the next street, and I climbed more stairs of a building decorated with our Union Jack, and this time was greeted by a giant Scot wearing a khaki shirt unbuttoned as far as it could be, its sleeves rolled above the elbow, and khaki shorts. When I explained who I was, he beamed a welcome.

"Oh, we know all about you, Lady Forrrtescue. We've been wondering when you'd turn up. You are ready to be flown home? You'd like to go straight through to Croydon, I expect?"

"Oh, *what* wouldn't I give to avoid another expensive wait in Paris — I dread that ghastly Metro — but my pass is stamped for a return to *Paris*, and at the airport they said, because of that, they could only fly me back to Paris," I answered sadly.

He looked at me with an ironical twist of the lips and muttered, "It's incredible — all that red tape about nothing," then sat down before a desk, scrawled a few words upon a slip of paper and handed it to me. A through ticket to Croydon.

"But you *can't* do that," I babbled. "You'll get into the most awful trouble — and so shall I. They said I *must* return *via* Paris — and they've been so wonderfully kind that —"

"I happen to be the Big White Chief," he astonishingly said as, with a twinkle, he handed me a thick cup of heavily sugared and very black tea. Now who would have thought it? But what a lovely bit of luck!

The R.A.F. hotel, to which I had been driven in the dark, proved to be in Martignagne — six kilometres *outside* Marseille — and we only reached it just before our last hint of petrol gave out. A measuring stick inserted in the tank on arrival had only a wet tip. Another half-mile and we should have been stranded. Another bit of luck.

A dreadful night of sticky heat and flies. The water supply of the hotel had given out, and there was none in lavatories or basins. The hotel servants were obliged to fill jugs and bowls from the tiny trickling fountain across the square, an added irritation to nerves already frayed by heat, flies and mosquitoes. The water supply was constantly being cut off now, they told me. Water was scarce after the drought, and also — there were the Americans who now occupied the whole coast and, as is the way of Americans, ceased not to wallow in baths by day and by night.

Lying uncovered on my bed I dripped and gasped for air. Misery. In the morning my tin of Nestlé's condensed milk, although sitting all night in a bowl of precious water, was cheese covered with a thick layer of drowned flies. Disgusting! The idea of floating up into clear cold air was heavenly, and with amusement I found myself longing to get back into an aeroplane, I who had been so fiercely prejudiced against them since their invention.

At the airport the same courtesy and quick efficiency, every man knowing his job and doing it with such quiet speed that I secretly agonised all the way home wondering if my baggage, which had been whisked away from me, really *had* been put into the plane, for I didn't see this done nor could I see any sign of it inside the plane. Only at Croydon did I discover that my small zip bags had been stowed away in a locker directly under my legs.

In company with a crowd of jocund sun-burned South African pilots, attired, as had been "The Great White Chief," only in shorts and open shirts, I roared up into the blue. Although they were so sketchily attired they didn't appear to feel cold, even at the highest altitude we reached, whereas I was glad to put on my uniform greatcoat and to cover my elderly knees with a rug. They were so excited by the prospect of seeing "The Mother Country" that they couldn't sit still. They prowled about the aeroplane; they frayed with pocket knives ropes that secured baggage to provide string to tie up those sinister paper-bags suspended above our heads which, as I have said, they filled with peaches for English relatives; they unpacked and repacked their duffle-bags, displaying to each other purchases, trophies and sentimental souvenirs; but when at last we sailed over the Channel and stared through white cotton-wool clouds (I used to resent that description as prosaic and bad, but cumulus clouds, seen from above, *do* look exactly like that), their restlessness and excitement increased tenfold. They asked our pilot to fly low over the shore-end of the famous petrol pipe-line which supplied the armies in France, and as we crossed Sussex wanted to be told about every big building, park or church spire. Here I could be informative.

Croydon at last, and we taxied gently down the runway to a halt. Stepping out of the aeroplane on to English soil and sniffing the smell of clover and a faint tang of the sea in the deliciously cool stiff breeze, I found myself murmuring "SAFE"; for though we are suffering post-war discomforts, scarcity of luxuries, heavy taxation, we are an organised, disciplined nation, and have never yet known what it is to lack good food. Our rations may be small, but we GET them. Coming from France where even the official monthly ration of *pâtés* (macaroni, spaghetti, vermicelli) sometimes came a month late — or not at all — and butter and fats were unknown, our English food seemed to me on my return from that hungry land to be lavish and satisfying beyond belief. No one who has not experienced it could ever realise the nervous feeling that lack of transport and all speedy means of communication with the outside world can give when living in an isolated spot. A kind of empty, dropping sensation in the pit of a tumpkin which is already nearly void.

I had experienced some such secret panic on arrival in Opio. Whether it was from fatigue, the transition from our chilly climate or the height at which we flew, I do not know, but I had blown up a temperature of 102.

Margharita had been terrified. How to get a doctor for *Madame*? She had no medicaments. "But some of your good vegetable bouillon will cure me, dear Margharita," I had assured her, and she hurried away to make it. When she had gone I had had a little private conversation with the Almighty.

"Look here," I said (very reverently and humbly). "I came out here to help Your unhappy children, big and small. I CAN'T be an additional burden upon them. There is so much to do that I CAN'T be ill here. Now — it's up to YOU."

And next morning my temperature had dropped to normal, and I had been given strength to carry out my programme.

CHAPTER
NINE

Heartbreak

Back at "Many Waters" there still lay ahead of me the toil of sending off all the stores for Provence and packing my personal possessions.

Old Nanny had been called to do higher work, and had been replaced by a South African "fan" of my books who volunteered to take charge of the cottage. Her cooking was, to say the least of it, extremely odd. Once she cooked and basted a piece of beef in what she imagined was Atora beef suet, thinking that the block of pale yellow substance within the box marked with this name was some new fat substitute. While shredding it and cooking the meat in it she never noticed that she had used YELLOW SOAP (packed in an Atora suet box so that it might not give a taste to the other rations delivered with it). She ate downstairs before I did and neither smelt nor tasted the soap — and she didn't die after that meal. Whereas I, after one mouthful, retired to the bathroom and very nearly did. Nor did I fully recover for some weeks. But I could overlook even a soapy meal because she adored my Blackness and took him for long wild walks while I toiled at my desk.

Old Romulus had had to be put to sleep, for he had

become dangerous to human beings and had bitten several persons who came to visit his mistress. That blow on the head besides blinding him had evidently also affected his brain and his nerves. My White Lady mourned him, an old tried friend and companion, and although he had made the life of my poor little Blackness less joyous than it would have been in such a dogs' paradise of woods and birds and rabbits, and mine, very often, a hell, I sorrowed with her, knowing so well the comfort the companionship of a loved dog can be. Henceforth Dominie was free to roam at will — red Rema often joined him in his expeditions in the woods — and they came back muddy and full of twigs — also of beans.

For him it was a very happy time, marred only by intervals of frustrated love. How boring men in love can be! Obsessed by one idea, losing their sense of humour and their appetite, and only wanting to find and be with the beloved one. The Blackness was like that at frequent intervals, feverish and restless; my care and affection became tiresome and superfluous to him, and he became a Bore with a capital B, poor little man, especially at night when he suddenly let forth blood-curdling howls and refused to be comforted. He had been in love, off and on, for weeks, disappearing for hours on end. Lately there had been a fascinating lady who lived several miles away, and to serenade her my little black troubadour must cross many dangerous main roads. Living in an olive grove on a mountain, he had never been trained to traffic, and when in this condition he hared off, looking neither to right nor left, making straight for his objective, so that we deemed it advisable to keep him on a lead for a time when we took him for walks.

One day I had to go up to London on business, returning in the evening. Before I began to descend my precipice I let forth my home-made yodel. Dominie would be listening for it, and if in captivity would be released so that he could rush off to meet me and bring me home in triumph. On this evening he came running towards me as usual, and then instead of jumping up at me and laughing in my face he sat down on the grass beside me and gave a terrible mournful little howl, looking at me beseechingly as though trying to confide some grief to me. Because of his lovesick condition during the past weeks, I tried to convince myself that it was merely the usual howl of frustration, yet my heart told me sickeningly that it was more than that. I had never before heard that note of intense sadness in his voice. I know now that it was his farewell to this lovely earth and to me. He KNEW. Then he climbed the rock to reach the old miller's trough, which was filled with stagnant water, dead leaves and had a film of paraffin floating on it as a precaution against mosquitoes. He drank thirstily of this horrible fluid before I could drag him away, and then started to tear up rough grass and weeds, which to my amazement he ate ravenously without making his usual careful selection. All this I attributed to unhappy love. Instead of going at once indoors I sat for a time on a wooden seat outside the cottage so that he could run free for a time under my eye. But after a languid visitation of his favourite rabbit holes he came and sat on the grass by my side as close to me as he could get. This, also, was unusual behaviour, for when out of doors on sporting bent, like all true men, he forgot the existence of women.

Feeling the air grow chilly and the grass become damp I went indoors, for once not preceded by The Blackness, who, instead of rushing up to my studio, after two ineffectual efforts jumped into a low armchair in the hall, looking at me piteously, shivering in every limb and with his teeth chattering. He was *ill* — he was having rigor. All night the most dreadful sickness and a raging thirst. There seemed nothing that I could do for him.

In the morning I sent for a vet. He said it was nothing, merely a chill. That was on Saturday. On Sunday morning Dominie was far, far worse, and I again telephoned urgently to the vet, who refused to come out because it was Sunday! I rang up another vet, who proved to have a heart. When he came he looked very grave. Turning up Dominie's soft lips he disclosed bright yellow gums — jaundice in an advanced stage. I didn't know that dogs had jaundice.

"Poor little fellow, he is desperately bad," he said sadly. "If treated at the onslaught of jaundice we can sometimes save them, but now — I fear I can hold out very little hope. If the bile gets into the bloodstream — septicaemia."

For two awful days and three interminable nights I never left my Blackness. I sat on the floor by his basket and tried to give him tiny drops of nourishment every two hours, holding him in my arms and heartening him when the attacks of sickness came and the little heart laboured so that he could hardly breathe. He only suffered terrible discomfort, not actual pain, and we fought together for his precious life. He was so gallant, so patient, and so lovingly grateful for my efforts to help him. On the third night I thanked him over and over again for his wonderful fidelity and love, and for his care of me, and I know that he understood and was a little comforted. But at dawn we lost the battle, and, as he left me, I called out loud for Elisabeth and Squibs to come and fetch him.

No one will ever know how much my little Blackness meant to me. We had shared so many things both bad and good, and he was Elisabeth's gift. He loved me with all his faithful brave little heart. He *always* understood. He was far, far more than a dog, and every one who knew him spoke of the sweetness and nobility of his character, and all feared for me if anything should happen to my Blackness.

Well — he had gone away, and was even now racing joyously with *Mademoiselle* and Squibs in the Elysian fields while I was left in a bitter desolation. Still, I could and did thank God for those years of perfect companionship, utter devotion and trust.

Perhaps He means His crusaders to stand alone and be of single mind and heart.

CHAPTER
TEN

Exit

Oh, the sadness and the exhaustion of that final exit from "Many Waters." I packed and sorted and destroyed, all day, every day, and for half the night, in a silent cottage becoming every day more denuded and less like home. Fine rain poured down insistently, and the grass-land around the cottage became more and more sodden, so that when each night I put on oilskins and started out for my climb up the cliff, laden with every kind of heavy package, my gum-boots made a squelching sound and were nearly pulled off my feet as I dragged them out of the soft ground. Every shrub was bowed down with heavy moisture, and as I butted my way through the over-arching boughs, streams of water cascaded over me and down my neck and face, and I had no free hand with which to wipe them. On every rock landing I was obliged to pause and regain my breath, then collect those awful suitcases or duffle-bags or knapsacks and toil onward and upward until I reached the cliff top and saw ahead of me the heartening lights of "The Kennels," and their tenant waiting to rub me down, fill me with hot soup and put me to bed. For the Lady of the Kennels had insisted that I should not sleep alone in my dismantled cottage, and had arranged her tiny guest-room for my use. She was the only person in England who understood and encouraged my decision to go back to France and share the hardships of my peasant friends. For years she had cherished the dream of a little house of her own in Provence, and was now determined to follow me out when conditions improved; for I had firmly refused to take out any helpers with me to face what every Frenchman I met warned me would be one of the hardest winters France had ever known.

Now the Lady of the Kennels, rather wistfully, did all she could to make the *déménagement* from "Many Waters" less grim, helping me to sort and to pack, emptying bulging cupboards (it is staggering the amount one can amass in five years) and swiftly abstracting and hiding any relics of my Blackness — collars, leads, feeding bowls, charcoal biscuits, balls — for HIS house was full of his possessions — before I should see them. She never knew that I was perfectly aware of these little tender acts of solicitude, but her swimming eyes or unnatural voice as she answered a question invariably betrayed her, for she had loved him too. Much experience in the caravan had developed her natural taste for cookery, and now she would leave me early to go to prepare something for our supper when I should at last appear in "The Kennels," gasping and spent. Without her I doubt if I could ever have achieved that awful departure. She was my strength and stay up to the final agony of boarding the boat train for Folkestone late at night, for the tide unkindly decreed that our boat must sail at dawn.

OH. . . ! My luggage (bluggage, as a friend of John's used to call it, you will know why). There were six large packages to be registered and five items of hand-luggage. The most cumbrous and formidable of this mountain was a gigantic duffle-bag to be described henceforth as The Sausage. This contained precious things for a fuel-less country — Alpine blankets, overcoats, rugs, an electric stove, a tiny electric breakfast cooker with oven and grill (this for Margharita to replace Heath Robinson), two electric boiling rings, and a typewriter. Could I ever transport that priceless Sausage safely to the South of France, I wondered. I had heard alarming stories of banditry on the French railways, and to those who had nothing left and could not replace anything from shops and factories denuded by the Boche, the contents of that Sausage represented, at that moment, thousands upon thousands of francs.

All my luggage was stencilled with the name of my fund, and marked by a seven-pointed star — but even so! This time I must make that weary journey by train. No possibility of being again adopted by the R.A.F. and transported magically to the Midi. The Sausage and his attendant Saveloys saw to that. This time I must cope entirely alone, and I confess that as I regarded those terrible packages I felt an oddly familiar sensation in the pit of my tumpkin always experienced on first nights or public platforms.

"Don't be an old funk-stick," I scolded myself inwardly. "Remember you are 'protected.' You're not making this little excursion for pleasure, God knows! And therefore He will look after you *and* the family of sausages, knowing that they are almost bursting with comforts for His children. Keep your chin up! Keep smiling! And all the other slogans you learnt in the war."

So with chin tilted deceptively high and a fixed elastic smile I got into my boat train and waved farewell to the Lady of the Kennels — and to England.

CHAPTER
ELEVEN

The Saga of the Sausage

It was nearly midnight when we reached our port of embarkation, which was swarming with American soldiers. A cold wild wind was blowing which threatened soon to reach gale force. We were all directed to a draughty and damp customs shed, and the queue of civilians and soldiers was so long that many unfortunates had to wait their turn outside in the wind and rain. I stood, surrounded by my five hand-packages, hoping that my legs would hold me up to the end. When my turn came I presented my credentials, and had the proud satisfaction of seeing all my things chalked without question, and I put back my unused keys into my handbag with a gusty sigh of relief, for many of those packages had been closed and strapped with the combined efforts of faithful Fred, the gardener, the Lady of the Kennels and myself. Heads, hands and tails had gone to the packing and CLOSING of those packages — and if opened again in a crowded customs shed. . . !

By the time I had crawled on board (at 1.30 a.m.) — for so great was the congested throng that one could only crawl — every place in the first-class saloon had been taken. Knowing that we were certain to have a terrible crossing, I decided to be really extravagant and to take a cabin, because though I am never seasick if lying flat, if I had to stay on the shelter deck in a chair all night — and the deck seemed already packed with occupied chairs — I knew that would mean disaster. The purser regretfully told me that every cabin was already taken, but seeing my grey curls, my uniform and perhaps the weariness of my expression when he broke this news to me, he again hurriedly scanned his bookings, and then said, "Well, Lady Fortescue, there is just one berth left in a six-berthed cabin, if you don't mind sharing it with some young American V.A.D.s."

Secretly I wondered how *they* would enjoy sharing it with *me*. This, to them, was doubtless an adventure, and my elderly presence might destroy the festive atmosphere in that cabin. I need not have feared. The five maidens, already undressed and clad in gay silken pyjamas, all paused in their evening hair-dressing operations to bestow a gleaming smile upon me, and with various joking remarks helped me to bestow my five hand-packages around my berth before sallying forth to "wash their teeth" in the ladies' cloak-room, which I, an old campaigner, had ascertained to be at the very end of the deck above us, and had already made use of before entering the cabin. Having learned the geography of the ship, and being sure of a very rough passage, I decided only to remove my uniform and shoes so that in any emergency I could quickly dress myself. Then I rolled myself in my blanket and, employing the sovereign prevention of seasickness recommended to me years ago, wedged baggage each side of me, put a heavy attaché case on my tumpkin to keep it steady when the ship should begin to roll, and in a few moments fell into a sound sleep.

In the small hours a sudden violent pitching and rolling told me that we were out at sea, but I was so tired that I didn't care what happened to us, and only heard the crashes of falling crockery, the bumping and sliding of baggage on the deck above, the howling of the wind and the smashing and suction of great waves in a kind of dazed dream, and was only thankful to be lying down. So that, until many hours later, I was unaware of the complete collapse of my five young companions, whose moans had been drowned by the noises caused by the seventy-five-miles-per-hour gale which had battered us all night. Oh, the poor lambs — what a piteous state they were in! All the assurance and gaiety of yesterday pitched and rolled out of them. I heard the senior girl recommending the only one of her charges with strength left to sit up, to go with her for a brisk walk on deck — a little dawn-patrol — as she'd been told that fresh air was the only prevention of seasickness. With wan and sickly looks those two brave survivors hoisted themselves from their berths, somehow dressed themselves and staggered out of the cabin. I wondered how soon they would come back as I followed the firm directions of my John: "Keep yourself warm. Lie flat. Shut your eyes." I had hardly had time to doze off again when the door burst open with a crash and two green-faced maidens, locked together, were precipitated into the cabin by a violent lurch of the ship. So far gone were they that we had the greatest difficulty in hoisting and heaving them back into their upper berths. The dawn-patrol had NOT been a success.

Half an hour before we were due to arrive I dressed, and rolled my way along to the ladies' cloak-room where, to my amazement and intense admiration, I found two little A.T.S. girls, stripped to the waist, scrubbing themselves with cold water and yellow soap! In public — and after such a night! In spirit I saluted the cleanliness of England, though I quailed from following that noble example. Retiring from the place after the lightest lick and polish, I felt rather ashamed of my lack of courage. However, little set-downs such as these are salutary to the soul. Seeing a queue of American soldiers about half a mile long waiting for breakfast, I decided that a stale beef sandwich devoured in the berth was preferable, and when I got back to it I started my strange *petit déjeuner* which, to my surprise, was very welcome and quite good. Looking up suddenly I became aware that one of the little Americans in an opposite berth was staring at me with an expression of mingled horror and amazement. Rolling her eyes around the cabin she pointed a languid finger at me, ejaculating:

"Say, gurrls! *Look* at that one!"

Helping those poor seasick maidens to divest themselves of their silk pyjamas, their hair-nets and other accessories of the elaborate toilet they had made *before* the ship began to roll was quite a business, and although we were nearly in port I didn't feel too good myself, for the cabin still swayed and its atmosphere was, to say the best of it, stuffy and vitiated. Then came the ordeal of disembarkation, not such a dignified proceeding as the long word implies, for progress was rather like a goose-step, high-stepping over hundreds of basins beside which drooped pallid American soldiers, all the bounce emptied out of them for once. The only sound one heard on those devastated decks was the oft-repeated ejaculation, "Oh, BOY!"

Thankfully I skidded down the wet gangway, and found myself once more upon — *not* dry land, for it was pelting with rain — but land. A porter, burdened with my hand-luggage, hustled me into the customs shed, where once more I passed triumphantly through without let or hindrance, and was soon comfortably installed in the train. I asked him if ALL my registered luggage had been put into the van. Yes, ALL, he assured me; and when I enumerated and described each package he lost patience, and said that if madame doubted his word she had half an hour before the train started to verify his words. The baggage vans were in front of the train, which appeared to be several miles long, and madame occupied the last Pullman. But cold and empty as I was, I could not relax during the long journey to Paris unless I had seen with my own eyes that The Sausage and all the Saveloys were travelling with me. So wearily I hoisted myself out of my comfortable seat and started the wet pilgrimage, buffeted by wind and rain.

I entered every luggage van, identified all the Saveloys, but — The Sausage, my so precious Sausage containing such priceless things, was nowhere to be seen! I questioned every railway official, describing my russet-red duffle-bag marked with a seven-pointed star and the name of the fund stencilled in black. No one had seen anything answering this description. Was it labelled? Yes, it had two huge tie-on labels. Like a frenzied rabbit I scuttled and scurried round, in between, and over mountains of American army baggage in search of my treasure, surely too gigantic to be overlooked, and suddenly, when all hope had nearly fled, I caught sight of a cylindrical *black* object lying neglected on the edge of the quay. Its shape was vaguely familiar, but its colour...! It WAS The Sausage, my dear, dear Sausage, but so sodden with sea-water that the stencilled star and address were no longer easily discerned. Crouching beside it I peered over its length, and then saw a drowned star and the ghost of a FORTESCUE. Both labels had disappeared — not even their strings remained, and I shall never be able to dismiss the certainty that they had been cut off and my Sausage segregated from the other luggage in the hope that in its soaked and darkened condition it would be unrecognisable and overlooked — as it so nearly was. I rushed to the luggage van, detached a label from a Saveloy (I always put on two labels in case of accidents), and attached it to The Sausage, which two burly porters then heaved into the van. Oh, dear! Should I ever get my Sausage safely to the South of France?

In Paris I was met by a very exquisite officer of L'Entr'aide Française who, having been given a description of grey curls, beret and dark blue uniform, identified me at once, and insisted upon shepherding me straight across the huge Gare du Nord and down the endless stone steps to his waiting car. I was surely tired and cold; if I would give him my baggage tickets for the registered luggage — six packages, I had said?

— he would see it safely into the *Consigne Militaire*, where it would remain during my short stay in Paris. Gratefully I got into the car and allowed him to cover me with rugs, and, with final injunctions about THE SAUSAGE, watched his long legs and patent leather feet twinkle up that long stairway and disappear.

After about twenty minutes he reappeared and, with a smiling bow, handed me my cloak-room ticket, assuring me that he had seen my SIX packages bestowed safely in the *Consigne Militaire*. Suffolk caution made me look at my ticket. Only FIVE objects were listed on it. This was sinister. It looked as though there were designs upon my Sausage. My escort swore that he had identified six packages on the barrow, but he agreed with me that we must both go back again and have the sixth package inscribed on the ticket, or of course I should never be able to claim it. The Sausage WAS there — and — *did* I detect a look of frustration upon the face of that French official as he changed the number 5 to 6 on my ticket? Second narrow escape.

Because I was in uniform a room had been engaged for me in the Hotel Bedford, reserved for English Services — and what a lovely room. Central heating, and a telephone beside a great French bed. Adjoining my bedroom a luxurious private bathroom, where almost boiling water poured forth at will by day and night. The Bedford was one of the few places in Paris where hot baths could be had at that time of fuel dearth. Good solid meals — more than I could eat — of American food. I stayed in that hotel for three days and three nights while I interviewed various French official bodies, and at the end of my visit my bill for all that comfort and good food, English efficiency and service was — five francs! Yes, five francs.

I stared in stupefaction at that bill, presented to me by the sergeant at the desk, then raised bewildered eyes to his, wherein there lurked a twinkle.

"Why five?" I enquired, with a lifted eyebrow.

"Seems unnecessary, don't it?" he answered, and we both laughed.

L'Entr'aide Française had lent me my "*Ange Gardien,*" as he styled himself, for the whole of my Paris visit, and he was indefatigable in his attentions, finding a free Entr'aide car with pain and effort to take me to my various destinations, and battling with the P.L.M. to get me a reserved seat and, if possible, a wagon-lit to take me to the South. On my last day he came to the hotel to inform me that a first-class seat, but, alas! no sleeper, had been reserved on the nine p.m. train to Cannes. This would enable me to have dinner comfortably before he arrived with a Ford van to collect me and my luggage. We must allow plenty of time to go and fetch the registered luggage from the Gare du Nord and to convey it to the Gare de Lyon, where it must be re-registered. In 1945 one could book tickets and luggage only as far as Paris.

I had still one more interview, which was arranged for half-past six in my hotel. I was sitting comfortably in the hall, smoking a cigarette at six-fifteen, when the revolving entrance doors suddenly revolved and whizzed with such speed and violence that the entrant was batted nearly into my lap. It was my "*Ange Gardien,*" no longer sleek and calm but with every feather ruffled by agitation.

79

"They have changed the train," he babbled in excited French. "We must start at once, for it leaves at seven o'clock."

"Then we've lost it already," said I, "for I must still pack my last-minute possessions, and then we must go to the Gare du Nord to collect the registered baggage, after which we cross Paris to the Gare de Lyon and re-register it. A physical impossibility in so short a time. I had better stay here for another night and leave to-morrow."

Hopping about and gesticulating wildly he informed me that L'Entr'aide had achieved the impossible and had secured a wagon-lit for me. He had already paid for it — the P.L.M. would never refund it. He had brought a Ford V.8, and we could certainly catch that train if I would only come quickly.

Well, miracles do happen, and perhaps with a postwar service this train might be late. I flew upstairs, hurled sponge, brushes, etc., into a zip bag, and in less than five minutes was back in the hall. An English sergeant handed me my thermos flask full of hot coffee, and a double ration of sandwiches, and in a few moments we were hurtling dangerously on our way to the Gare du Nord. I myself superintended the extraction of Sausage and Saveloys, but it is never a quick matter to identify and get out baggage from any cloak-room, and a *Consigne Militaire* is more overcharged than most. It all took precious time, and when we at last arrived at the Gare de Lyon, driving at breakneck speed, it was already ten minutes to seven.

Needless to say, the registration office was already closed — as I had anticipated. Wearily I suggested a return to the Bedford. But I reckoned without the impetuosity of French guardian angels. Mine had already hailed no less than six porters, commanding them to seize the registered luggage and run. I had a dazed vision of two underfed little Frenchmen staggering along carrying The Sausage between them, while the other four trotted after them carrying Saveloys. My *"Ange Gardien"* packed hand-baggage under his wings and I seized what he couldn't carry. Breathlessly we panted after the porters the whole length of that interminable train (the wagon-lits were, of course, in front), while interested passengers regarded us from its windows thinking no doubt that I owned a travelling circus.

Arrived at the door of my sleeper the attendant — very naturally — refused to allow so much baggage into a Pullman car. We must take it to the luggage van. Thereafter the air was rent with explanations, execrations, lamentations; then to my horror I saw my escort wave commands to that army of sweating porters, who rushed the attendant, overpowered him by sheer force of numbers and the bulk of their freight, which they hurled into the corridor. I was violently propelled from behind, and found myself embracing The Sausage, and had merely time to throw a handful of notes from the window to those poor exhausted men and — we were off. The last vision I had of my *"Ange Gardien"* he was standing white-faced but triumphant in the posture of a general who has won his battle. But I was left alone to face the enemy.

Punctured though I felt I had yet to summon every effort to subdue the hostility of the officials of the train, by explanations, pathos and smiling apology, although seething with rage at having been placed in such a position. While I talked the attendant was silently pushing and heaving that mass of bluggage, which entirely blocked the corridor, into my wagon-lit. Eleven packages in all — counting hand-luggage. Would there be room for me when it was all bestowed? I doubted it. I remunerated him heavily when he had done the best he could, and then I writhed my way into the carriage. The Sausage stood proudly on end in the middle of it — Saveloys were piled in the racks and on my berth and upon the *lavabos*, but I thought I could manage to undress and slide into a strip of the berth. It was then that I got the worst shock of all. In the farthest corner of the compartment, peering at me through an aperture between bluggage, was the empurpled face of a furious little Frenchman. So embedded in my luggage was he that I hadn't noticed him. What was he doing in my wagon-lit, anyway? Pushing The Sausage irritably to one side, he asked me with awful calm HOW he was to *faire sa toilette* with The Sausage blocking the way to the *lavabos* and Saveloys sitting *on* it? Then he glared at me and made an expressive gesture which clearly said, "Answer me THAT."

Despairingly I insisted that a first-class sleeper had been booked for me, and the number of my reservation corresponded with that on the door of the wagon-lit. To prove it I produced my ticket. He produced his and poked it through the aperture under my eyes. The same number. But my place was marked (very appropriately) 13 and his was 14.

A DOUBLE WAGON-LIT, and I had got to share it WITH A MAN. . . ! And what a man! Nothing romantic about a little round paunch, a bald head and pince-nez pinching a red swollen nose, for the poor little man was suffering from a violent cold in the head. I was sorry for him. The sudden intrusion of me and my bluggage was enough to extinguish any spark of *entente cordiale* that might hitherto have smouldered in his breast, but I was also sorry for myself. To pay an enormous price for a first-class sleeper and then be obliged to share it — with that man.

An explanation of the contretemps was due, and I succeeded in calming him, although he still muttered about the impossibility of washing and shaving himself next morning with so much luggage blocking his path. Then I went in search of the attendant. Surely there was some mistake? I had never heard of a *double* first-class wagon-lit. Sleeping cars had only just been added to the trains, I was informed. There were very few of them, and every one travelling South demanded them, therefore it was necessary to pack as many people into them as possible. I suggested that surely the *Monsieur* travelling with me might be exchanged for a lady, but this, it seemed, was also impossible. The attendant, in spite of my heavy tip, waxed impatient — he had beds to make up and *le bon Dieu* only knew how he was going to make up the beds in my compartment with all that obstructing baggage — and if he put it into the corridor it would block travellers from reaching the dining-car. I was in a very delicate position, for I knew well that my bluggage ought to be in the van, and that by throwing it into the Pullman my *"Ange Gardien"* had broken P.L.M. law. There was nothing for it but to swallow that little Frenchman. Fortunately he went to the restaurant car for his dinner, while I remained in the wagon-lit, ate my hefty English sandwiches and washed the wedges down with coffee. Then when the attendant had, after much heaving and mountain climbing of baggage, at last succeeded in making up the beds, I locked the door and got into mine, having removed only my uniform tunic, beret and shoes. When my fellow traveller returned I would feign sleep, while he achieved that *toilette* he seemed determined to make. I had made all that I intended to make in such company.

That poor little Frenchman — I had a profound pity for him — dallied as long as he could in the restaurant car, but at last was obliged to return to his overcrowded compartment. At last he entered, stood in the doorway snuffling and polishing his pince-nez (my back was turned to him but I could see his reflection only too clearly in the polished wood flanking my berth), then he cast a nervous look at me but seemed reassured by my apparently somnolent back, squared his shoulders and then took off — first his collar and tie, then his waistcoat and shoes, then his shirt — I tried *so* hard not to watch these proceedings, but one of my eyes *would* open — unpacked a pyjama jacket and put it on, then looked — downward — rather doubtfully. I shut my eyes tightly — would he, oh, would he take — THEM off? Next I heard a thud — the placing of the ladder up which he must climb to reach the upper berth. The long-suffering Sausage, more sinned against than sinning, lurched against me, and I felt the impact of my precious electric cooker upon my stern, and even at that moment could rejoice that it was still there, not yet stolen, and, opening startled eyes, was just in time to see two fat TROUSERED legs disappearing into the upper berth. So — he HADN'T. The rest of his *toilette* was, mercifully, made in privacy on the top shelf — not an easy feat it seemed by the frenzied scuffling and bumping overhead. Suddenly THEY were flung into the air, the light was extinguished, and after a very short time snorts, stertorous snores, interrupted at intervals by raucous choking fits, proclaimed that my companion had fallen into a troubled sleep. Poor little man. Not a very fascinating citizen.

My decision to rise before anyone was awake and make *my* toilet in the public *lavabos* in the corridor would have kept me awake even had I not been too overtired and anxious to sleep. Very early indeed next morning I crept out of my berth, put on shoes and tunic and, clasping my dressing bag, slid out into the corridor. It was bitterly cold, before sunrise — but we were nearing the South where almost certainly the sun *would* rise. Only the blue-chinned attendant unwashed and unshorn, sprawled in the little box reserved for his use. He opened heavy eyes to stare at the mad Englishwoman, then with an effort rose to his feet to start another day's work. It isn't easy to wash satisfactorily when the plug of the basin is lost and the only way to get water is to keep a finger firmly pressed upon a button-tap which, if released, promptly shuts off the supply, but I did manage to remove some of the smuts of the journey and to comb my tangled curls. Emerging, I asked the attendant in which direction lay the restaurant car, as I would like my *petit déjeuner*. He informed me that the restaurant car had been taken off during the night, but offered me his own tin mug in which was some black fluid. I had to *try* to drink it — my first experience of that nauseating bitter substitute for coffee, made from acorns and goodness knows what else. I would return to the wagon-lit and put on my greatcoat, for I was shivering with cold — but I found that I was *locked out*! My little Frenchman was making *his toilette*, and had evidently decided that difficult as it must be his discomfort should be seen by none. He took at least an hour over it while I shivered in the corridor, feeling miserable, unable to reach greatcoat or sandwiches, and bruised by the lurching and bumping of the train.

First-class travelling de luxe, complete with wagon-lit, I reflected a trifle bitterly.

When he did at last open the door the poor man was in a better humour, refreshed no doubt by that long *toilette*. He could even make some feeble little jokes on how he had contrived to achieve the operation by piling Saveloys into a corner, putting The Sausage in a horizontal position and kneeling upon it to shave, and so on. Then he went in search of his non-existent *petit déjeuner*, and was doubtless also consoled by a swig of that nauseating and bitter concoction from the tin mug of the attendant. During his absence a train official came along the corridor informing all passengers that they must alight at Marseille, as the train went no farther.

Alight at Marseille. . . ? My ears, though uncommonly

sharp, must have deceived me. My ticket was marked CANNES. In trepidation I pursued him, and my enquiries were answered by the information that there were no wagon-lits on the through train to Cannes, only on the train to Marseille. All passengers for Cannes must get out and await the arrival of the Cannes train which left Paris nightly at nine p.m. The train in which it had originally been arranged that I should travel! It would arrive packed with people and with no reserved seat, and I should almost certainly have to huddle in the over-crowded corridor — much hated because of my five pieces of hand-luggage. And while waiting for the train to arrive I must re-register the heavy packages. What a nightmare! For I had been warned not to leave any luggage for one moment unprotected in any station.

At Marseille not a porter in sight and the cloak-room half a mile away! Seeing an immaculate first-class Frenchman nonchalantly pushing a trolley down the platform towards the luggage van, in desperation I approached him and pleaded for the hospitality of his enormous trolley for my luggage also. He paused, adjusted an eyeglass in a very keen dark eye, smoothed his pointed beard, fingered the white carnation in his button-hole while eyeing the badges of Général de Gaulle and of the French Red Cross in my lapel. Then, with a flash of white teeth and a beautiful bow he introduced himself as *le Docteur X, Specialiste de Nice*, and very much at my service. I poured forth the story of my unfortunate journey and the distressing muddle over my ticket, whereupon he informed me that as a first-class passenger to Cannes I had the right to be transported there by a magnificent Autocar awaiting us now outside the station and large enough to contain — even *my* luggage (said with a twinkle). Doubtless if I looked inside my ticket book I should find the pink slip authorising me to finish my journey in this way. He extracted those of himself and his wife to show me. But my luck was completely out — there was no pink slip inside my ticket book. In the words of the poem "someone had blundered" — and blundered badly. All he could do he did. Together we heaved The Sausage and its retinue on to the trolley, and together we trundled it along that interminable platform to the luggage cloak-room. On the way there he asked me why I had come out to France at such a moment (a question that in moments of cowardice I had been asking myself). I told him what I was trying to do — what I intended to do — and he offered me his services and co-operation should I need them. Then his wife hailed him, and once again I was alone.

I found a sulky, underfed little porter who seemed to think my luggage excessive for one woman, so I had to explain what it contained. I told him that, later on, one hundred and eight huge cases of clothes and comforts for the children of Provence would be following me out, and then a look of interest transformed his thin face. He had five *gosses*, three boys and two girls, if *Madame* should be able to spare a garment or two — perhaps *shoes*? Life was so hard and there was nothing to be bought, even if one had money to buy clothes for the children. I asked their ages and sizes. I produced a notebook and, leaning up against the sympathetic Sausage, wrote down his name and address and all details of his children, even to their size in shoes. I promised not to forget him, and when the time came I did not. Now he became all eager enthusiasm for my mass of luggage, and when the one hundred and eight cases arrived he would make them his special care. If *Madame* would stay outside with her hand-packages, he would go and register the heavy stuff. I felt that I could trust him, and presently he returned with the slip upon which all *six* of my packages were inscribed.

Soon afterwards the Cannes train came steaming in. My apprehensions were only too well founded. Never have I seen so overcrowded a train. The corridors were packed with struggling humanity, but my little porter fought his way inside to see if he could find a vacant seat for me. Nothing. Nothing at all except one Pullman reserved for American forces containing only one G.I. pensively lolling alone. My porter assured me that, being in uniform, I had the right to travel in this Pullman, and seeing an American A.P.M. I accosted him.

"What's bitin' yew, ma'am?" he asked me irritably, and, when I explained my predicament, said I must go to the American "boorow" at the other end of the station. When I protested that the train would start in a few moments he merely shrugged his shoulders and moved off, and my little porter, with a despairing gesture, started pushing my packages into the corridor between the legs of enraged passengers. Some railway official shoved me inside after them, I threw a note to my little porter, and the train started. Very much like my departure from the Gare de Lyon the night before — but worse, oh, far worse! My suitcase had been placed upon that awful telescopic platform which connects the carriages and writhes with the motion of the train. I perched on its edge, banked in with luggage and hot humanity, and was revolved from right to left as we progressed. I found that the people surrounding me were part of a pilgrimage returning from Lourdes — sick people shepherded by nuns. The Reverend Mother, tears of weariness and humiliation trickling down her face, was throned in the *cabinet* opposite me, its door wedged open by a mountain of packages. She sat upon her strange throne with perfect dignity, her eyes closed, her lips moving in prayer as she fingered her rosary. In the corridor the poor little nuns forgot their own misery in their selfless way as they tried to mitigate that of their suffering pilgrims. From pathetic little paper bags they brought forth fragments of dry *biscottes* to feed them, and wetted their lips with water, propping lolling heads on haversacks. The stench of those poor people in that hot atmosphere was indescribable, explained in some measure by a tragic-faced little Sister, who whispered to me in an anguished voice, *"On n'a pas pu s'évacuer depuis Toulouse, Madame."*

Waves of nausea and faintness nearly swamped me at intervals. I had had no breakfast and a great deal of agitation, but as I was too tightly wedged I could not move my arms to fumble in my bag to see if a sandwich still remained — even if I could have swallowed it in such an atmosphere — but I could have given it to those exhausted people. I kept control of mind and body by saying to myself sternly: "This is VERY good for you. You, for four short hours, are enduring a very little part of the misery the French have been enduring for years. You wanted to share their hardships. Well, this is one of them."

I did endure till the end without disgracing myself, but those four hours of complete discomfort seemed like four days, enlivened though they were by various comic-tragic incidents when passengers, having stepped over and stamped upon me and my fellow travellers in the effort to reach the *cabinet*, found there the Reverend Mother, throned in state, and turned muttering away. One irate and determined Frenchman actually succeeded in displacing her temporarily, but being unable to shut the door behind him because of the mass of packages within, which for lack of space could not be placed elsewhere, obeyed the commands of nature in full view of us all.

Cannes AT LAST! Oh, thank God for His sunshine, blue sky and fresh air. Soon, soon I should be safely home again in my little "Sunset House," and this late purgatory would seem an evil dream. Now to find a *camion* (lorry) to convey me and my bluggage to my mountain top. Taxis were extinct, and as no one here knew the day upon which I should be travelling, no Red Cross car could meet me. I found a *camion* outside the station, bargained with the driver to take me to Opio for one thousand francs (a cheap rate for those days), and asked my porters to load in the luggage. They put in my hand-packages and went in search of the registered stuff. They were gone a very long time and returned, scratching their heads and gesticulating.

My registered luggage was not there. My own frantic and exhaustive search, for I refused to believe in such a misfortune, proved that they were right in saying that it had not been put in at Marseille. It would come in a luggage train perhaps in a week or a fortnight's time. . . !

I had already hired this enormous *camion* to transport The Sausage and its entourage to Opio. It would now be necessary to hire yet another to collect my stuff when — and IF — it came. Marseille had an evil reputation for theft, and my defenceless Sausage, with its so precious contents, would now have every chance of being pilfered, unless the little hungry porter protected it; for the railway officials had evidently prohibited him from loading more luggage into already overcrowded vans.

I must just trust in Providence and the porter, and in the meantime, if I didn't get home soon, put food into my empty body, and then wash it and put it to bed, I felt that I should surely collapse. Only one more test of endurance — the drive in the *camion* to Opio. There was a seat beside the loquacious driver, and on my other side was a kind of kitchen stove which he filled with fuel and which nearly roasted me. Half suffocated by fumes and dust, deafened by the roar of the engine and the screaming of the driver, who, in true friendly Provençal fashion, ceased not to yell all the details of his family life into my ear as we thundered up the mountains, bumped and bruised by the jolting over rocks and ruts, at last we reached the haven where I would be.

HOME again — and this time I had come back to stay. My visa was marked *"rentrer en domicile,"* a lovely finality about that. The welcome of Margharita, the warm peace of an October afternoon, the scent of late roses, the distant mountains veiled in lilac mist, and the smoke of autumn bonfires mounting and swirling in clouds of azure blue above the silver olive groves. Yes, this was HOME.

I had arranged with my charioteer that when my bluggage should arrive from Marseille he would collect it and bring it to me. Proudly he reeled off a list of *personnalités*, many of them English, whom in the past he had faithfully served. That was all that I could do. Margharita bewailed the lack of her promised electric cooker. Surely, most surely, would such a priceless treasure be stolen.

But, after eight days of apprehension, The Sausage and the Saveloys arrived INTACT.

CHAPTER
TWELVE

Hey Diddle Diddle

Now began the comedy, or shall we call it farce (because to me there is something farcical in all officialdom, especially perhaps in France) of renewing *carte d'identité* and procuring *carte d'alimentation*. Although I was present in the flesh, grasping my old *carte d'identité*, the equivalent of our English passport, and had lived in France since 1930, so was known by all, I found that my flesh could not be nourished until my identity had been proved again and my *carte d'identité* renewed, with a fresh set of photographs taken in profile and exposing the left ear because, although resident in France, I was an *étranger*. Why, oh why, was that wonderful offer of Mr. Churchill's, made at the moment of France's greatest peril, that France and England should be as one nation, sharing all resources, dropping all barriers and formalities, not accepted? WHY cannot that offer be made again! Now I must submit to all the tiresome regulations affecting "aliens" in France.

My little Grey Pigeon had not yet arrived, and I could NOT face travelling in the only bus to Nice, even if by lucky chance I could find standing room inside it. The atmosphere of that bus baffled description, but all the odours therein — garlic, hot unwashed bodies and clothes — were surpassed by the terrible stench of what was called petrol. Passengers with their luggage or shopping bags, men, women and children were clotted together on the seats or stood, pressed flat into each other like dates or figs packed for export, swaying *en masse* with every lurch of the mined-at-intervals road which had only been hastily and temporarily repaired, unable to extricate a steadying arm. Very few survived the atmosphere combined with the swaying and bumping of the bus, and when overcome with nausea could not escape to privacy and the outer air. Margharita had told me all about it, begging her Madame not to attempt such a journey. Then *how* could I get to the Préfecture of Nice, where the Opio officials had assured me that I must apply? I toiled up to our small Mairie perched on a little round mountain opposite mine. At its foot I accosted a handsome young man with dark intelligent eyes in a very brown face, and asked him if I should find *Monsieur le Maire* at the *Mairie* at that hour? Sweeping off his beret with one hand, and with the other tapping his chest as he sketched a bow, he said:

"*Lui-même, Madame.*"

"But you're much too young to be a mayor," I protested. "You ought to have a long white beard."

"*Cependant je suis père de famille*," he laughed, and then, with pride, began to talk of his splendid boy and girl, the happiest topic of all in France where love of the family, *la famille*, transcends and glorifies all else.

Our mayor was elected after the liberation by the Resistance, of which he had been part. I liked him instantly, straight and true, with no *chi-chi* about him. When we entered the *Mairie* he attended to all in their turn, and since I was a late-comer I took my place at the end of the row of chairs occupied by waiting peasants, and I watched, with admiration, the kind and patient way he dealt with these simple people, many of whom could neither read nor write. He did this for them, reading over documents relating to laws or boundaries or privileges, sometimes three times over, to be sure that they understood, showing them, if they approved, where to affix their mark in place of signature before he stamped the paper with the official seal of the *Mairie*, and signed his own name as *Maire*. If he had offered the lady of Domaine de Fort Escu precedence of these peasants I should have refused it, but to each in their rightful turn he gave his patient, undivided attention. The right man in the right place, rightly respected and, as I learned later, liked by all. He owned the olive mill in the valley where every one took their olives to be crushed, and had grown rich and influential, but remained unspoiled. We are very proud of our mayor, and I count him now as one of my best friends.

When at last my turn came, he told me that I must go to Nice to go through all the foolish formalities. He apologised with a wry smile. Alas! he could not save me from them, but when I expressed my horror of the motor-bus, said he could — and would — drive me into Nice next day, where he had official business, if I could be ready at eight o'clock in the morning.

Eight o'clock, and my treatment to do before we started! But any effort was preferable to a journey in that awful motor-bus which, for me, could end only in ignominious disaster, and so I very gratefully accepted this offer, and was driven to Nice.

At the Préfecture they took charge of my old *carte d'identité*, and after smelling it over very suspiciously handed me a food card giving me the right to draw rations for one week only. This must be stamped by the Opio *Mairie and renewed each week at Nice*! What nonsense in a country with scarcely any transport! Opio is about forty kilometres from Nice.

When I took my miserable card back to the *Mairie* at Opio, the old secretary who gives out the monthly food tickets looked over his spectacles at me for a moment in silence and then snorted indignantly, "*IMBECILES,*" as he swiftly changed the date of renewal on my card to a month later, and gave me food tickets for a month! That refreshed me. Snip the restricting red tape and do the sensible if illegal thing. Now I was dealing with a true Provençal, and his action made me feel cosy and at home once more. I never visited the Préfecture at Nice again on this subject, and each month, ever since, my food card has been renewed with those of the other inhabitants of Opio.

But even the monthly food cards were a farce, because there was hardly ever any food to be got with the tickets. In 1945 the official monthly rations sometimes didn't come in until nearly the end of the following month, and a small announcement in the local newspaper then told us what we were entitled to get — *pâtés*, sometimes a little sugar and a block of a white fat-substitute called *Vegetaline* made, it was alleged, from nuts. But such tiny quantities were allowed, and butter, fish and meat were never seen. The small quantity of milk produced by the few cows of the neighbourhood was rightly reserved for the children.

During the Battle of Britain *Mademoiselle* had bought half a cow which, for obvious reasons, she named "London Pride." The other half of "London Pride" was owned by a peasant who had walked miles to a cattle market, bought her and driven her home in triumph to the château. *Mademoiselle* fed, housed and had all the responsibility for the cow, and never quite seemed to obtain her fair share of its milk, so in the end she bought out "Simple Simon," as, in her letters, she called the peasant (*not* very appropriately, as it had proved), and became "London Pride's" sole proprietor. The milk was a boon to all her poor neighbours as well as to Elisabeth and her companion. When I came out in June I was assured that I should have milk from "London Pride" when I returned for good in October. But when I did arrive "London Pride" was in calf, and could only supply enough milk for the inhabitants of *Mademoiselle*'s château.

Whenever they went away, as they frequently did, the care of the cow was entrusted to my Margharita. This meant leading it out on the terraces of the olive grove and tethering its long chain to a tree so that it could strive to find something edible in the dried up vegetation beneath it. As there was scarcely anything for poor "London Pride" to find, her place must be changed about every twenty minutes to half an hour, which meant towing her from terrace to terrace up rocky paths, always anxious lest she slip over a wall, break a leg and lose the precious expected calf which if safely born would fetch thousands of francs. If it began to rain heavily, "London Pride" must be collected, led back to her stall in the château stable and rubbed dry. This performance had to be repeated constantly, for the moment the sun came out again it was important to take the poor beast to pasture. There was little hay for her in the stable, it cost twenty francs a kilo (2 lbs.), and could be got only from the high mountains — and there was no transport to bring it down.

One day Margharita went off for the day to try to find some bran for her three skinny hens, and I was left in charge of "London Pride." Although country-bred I had never had the personal care of a cow, and I viewed this responsibility with some apprehension, though I would have died rather than disclose my fear to Margharita. She warned me that the cow had become rather *méchante* of late, no doubt owing to her condition, and I must be careful of her horns and *heels*, and beware lest she took to them suddenly and tried to break away from me — and IF she should stampede I must on no account let her fall over a wall and damage herself. At dusk she must be led back to her stable — and she wouldn't want to go; she would try every trick on me, especially as I was strange to her. Once inside the stable she must be tied up near the manger, but doubtless she would first try to escape. Madame must go inside with her and quickly shut the door.

Margharita did not particularise what would happen then. With every warning she gave me (in a light and bantering way, for she rather enjoyed the antics of that temperamental cow) my heart grew heavier, and by the mischievous gleam in her huge eyes I think she divined this.

When she had fed her hens, got through her other duties and departed, I braced myself for the ordeal. When I funk a thing I make myself do it at once, and I did funk the responsibility of this strange cow. Wearing ancient trousers the better to climb walls and scramble about terraces, and armed with a stout ash stick, I descended the mountain to Elisabeth's château feeling very sure that somewhere or other she was laughing at me. Inside the stable "London Pride" eyed me with the deepest suspicion, but as she was longing to get out she allowed me to loosen her halter, fix her long chain and lead her forth. Once outside she hurried her steps, and I perforce had to hurry mine. We went out of the courtyard at a trot, which soon quickened into a canter. Lolloping along behind her I devoutly hoped that it would not develop into a wild gallop, for at all costs I must not let go that chain, and the day was hot.

She chose her own terrace. I had no say in the matter, but was glad that the selected terrace was on *my* property, for I had to change her place every half-hour. She began to graze, and I wound the chain round an olive tree, giving her as much latitude as possible. I was thankful she had chosen a low terrace, for its supporting wall was less dangerous, and grateful also that there seemed to be a certain amount of edible grass under the olive trees within her reach, so that I could, with conscience, leave her there for thirty minutes. Divide your day into half-hours, from nine a.m. till six p.m., and you will then realise that no less than eighteen times did I descend my many terraces from the house, unwind that chain, lead (or be led by) a protesting or over-eager cow to another terrace, and then climb the steep ascent back to the house, where more work of Margharita's must be done. If I have glossed over details of those changing of positions it is because the relation of that cow's antics and the various surprises she gave me would become boring if recounted eighteen times. *Méchante* she was, and I knew that she gloried in my inexperience and mocked my misadventures, all deliberately caused by her. I would unloose the chain and give it a gentle pull to inform her that we were now in search of pastures new. She would follow with perfect docility for a few seconds and then suddenly race ahead of me, nearly jostling me over a wall as she passed and wrenching my arm nearly out of its socket as she rounded an olive tree and turned in her tracks, making straight for me with horned head lowered. I could never have believed that a cow could be agile enough to tie herself and me into such knots with that long chain, or that at my age I could perform such skipping and dodging antics. She exercised me well, did "London Pride," and I was very thankful when dusk fell and the hour of her bedtime had arrived. But the worst moment of all had also come, for Margharita's warnings had thickened as night fell. Would it be *very* cowardly to seek the aid of the guardian of the Castello, a little British sergeant lacking one hand? He, being a Cockney, would know even less about cows than I did, but his presence would give me moral if not physical support. I went down to the château to see if I could collect him. Yes, he was there. As I had anticipated, he knew nothing of cows and had never seen this one put to bed, but he would come with me and lead her by the chain while I followed behind with my stick to head her back if she turned, and to give her, as Margharita had counselled, a gentle dig in the flank to urge her towards her bedroom.

I unloosed the chain and put it in his one hand, and he started to descend the steep rocky little path which cut mid-way through the terraces. Greatly daring, I poked the cow in the stern as advised by Margharita. The result was as unexpected as it was shattering.

Hey diddle diddle! Was she trying to jump over the moon?

Enormous as she was, she suddenly bucked like a broncho, then kicked her back legs skyward and — made off at a gallop downhill.

In a flash the slack chain tautened and the poor sergeant, who had wound it round his wrist for security, gave a yelp of pain, was towed along for a moment, then *let go*. The suddenly liberated cow hurtled down the mountain, leaping every boulder but miraculously never stumbling. In those agonising seconds I saw the wreck of all my tender care. She would CERTAINLY break one, if not all, of her legs; her calf would be prematurely born and still-born; every one would be heart-broken. I turned tragic and horrified eyes towards the sergeant, crying, "Oh, we've *lost* her!"

I had raced after the cow with the wild idea of catching her, so that I had not seen what happened to him when the chain was whipped from his wrist and he, too, was liberated. Of course as he was throwing his weight backwards as he and the cow raced downhill, he fell with a bump on his stern. And there he still sat in paroxysms of laughter — in which I had to join.

"*She's* all right, your ladyship," he reassured me between gasps. "She's had her bit of fun and now she'll make for home an' bed. I bet we'll find her in the courtyard of the château." And sure enough we did, looking as though the butter which could be made from her milk — when she had any — wouldn't melt in her mouth.

"Now I'll hand over to you, my lady," said the sergeant. "It's a wonder she didn't break me wrist with her pranks, and me one hand is useful to me."

I had now a strong distrust of "London Pride," and her present demeanour didn't deceive me in the least.

"Stay for a bit, sergeant," I pleaded. "When — and if — I get her into the stable, Margharita warns me that she'll try to do a bolt. The moment we get inside slam the door after us and bolt it, will you?"

I shortened the chain and pulled her into the stall. Only just in time the sergeant slammed and bolted the lower door, for she suddenly turned and charged it with all her weight. Finding her effort to escape foiled, she backed into her narrow stall. *Backed . . . !* Now how was I to turn her round so that she faced her manger and attach her horns by the chain swinging from it? Because of her abnormal size it seemed a physical impossibility for her to turn, even if I could induce her to do it.

At this juncture the sergeant, grinning over the door as he realised my predicament, had an inspiration.

"I'll go and fetch the wife," he said. "She was born on a French farm, and she'll know what to do."

She did. Fetching a juicy cabbage from her kitchen, she climbed up into the loft above the stable, opened a trap door and dangled the fresh greenery above the manger, making cooing sounds to the cow. "London Pride" turned her head, looked upward, saw the cabbage, looked and longed.

Slowly she tried to revolve, while we watched anxiously as she twisted and sidled — and stuck. But at last she achieved it, and her head was then where her wicked tail had been. The cabbage dropped with a flump into the manger, and while "London Pride" quietly munched I, guided by instructions from the smiling woman still peering through the trap door, secured the cow by the chain, and made a thankful exit from the stable. I thanked that kind couple for their help, and climbed the mountain for the last time that day.

When Margharita came home I had had time to change my clothes and cool down.

"*Et la vache?*" she immediately asked, with rather a cheeky look in her eyes.

"*Elle va très bien,*" I said casually, then changed the subject to her adventures that day. But I'm sure she listened with glee to the story recounted by the guardians of the château on the morrow, though she tactfully never referred to them.

CHAPTER
THIRTEEN

All Souls' Day

All Souls' Day dawned sadly in quiet rain, as it so often does in Provence, as though the skies also wept for the dear departed.

I lit candles in my little chapel for all my beloveds, and put a fresh spray of rosemary in the collar of my Blackness.

I had not yet had the courage to make that one sad pilgrimage to our tiny village cemetery where they had laid Elisabeth on the little mountain opposite the château. I knew that only her lovely body lay there, and that her still lovelier spirit was having a marvellous time somewhere else, yet somehow I dreaded that pilgrimage.

But on All Souls' Day I would go in the evening when all the people of the village carrying their chrysanthemums had tended their graves. I wanted to be alone with her and memory, but Margharita, who had loved *Mademoiselle*, begged to be allowed to accompany me. She had seen me fitting a candle into a beautiful old lantern of pierced iron, the design of holes forming a star, which Elisabeth once gave to me. She knew that I intended to light it and place it at the head of *Mademoiselle*'s grave, as is the custom of Provence on All Souls' Night. How often had Elisabeth and I watched the tiny flickering lights of these candles from the wall of her secret garden, a lovely mysterious sight against the background of dark cypress trees which bordered the cemetery.

She had asked in her will that when she died she should be buried on her own property, between one of her own great cypresses and the green enclosure near the studio where she kept her rabbits. "So cosy, Pegs!" she had said to me when telling me of her wish. But during the war this was impossible, and she was carried to the lovely little Opio cemetery where now I was going with Margharita.

No stone as yet marked the place, but a mason who loved her (and who did not?) had carted rocks from her own land and built a low rustic wall round the grave; another loving hand had sown green grass, and the enormous V was there, marked out in the old-fashioned double white pinks from my garden, the little *mignardises*.

Our pilgrimage was made at dusk. The pouring rain had discouraged the peasants from lighting their candles, so that when I lighted hers it shone alone amid the white flowers that I had gathered from her garden and from mine. From the head of her resting-place could be seen her beloved château flanked by the two gigantic grey-stemmed cypresses which stood at the end of the secret garden, the garden of the monks. Seen through the rain it was all grey and soft, the silvery olive trees shimmering as the wind turned their leaves. The village children had made a cross of Lorraine for *Mademoiselle* with the heads of flowers, for she had been one of the true Resistants, refusing even in the blackest hours of the war to admit even the possibility of defeat, or to allow pessimism among the peasants.

"*A la Victoire!*" she had cried gaily. She had conquered pain, and I knew that she would fight with me to conquer despair and disease among the children of the people she loved.

As I knelt for a moment by her resting-place it seemed to me, as I sent the prayers of my heart to God and my thoughts to her, that I heard her gaily cry:

"*A la Victoire, Pegs!*"

CHAPTER
FOURTEEN

Remaking a Home

While waiting for the arrival of my one hundred and eight cases of clothes and comforts from England I got all the relief organisations, the mayors of towns and villages, the school teachers, priests and doctors to give me lists of the really necessitous families, with the names, age, sex and complete measurements of each child. I was so anxious to equip them with warm clothing before the cold weather came, and the winters of late years had been exceptionally severe, frost even freezing into a solid cake the twenty thousand litres of water in the *bassin* near my house.

These preliminaries took time, but less time than I had anticipated, for the misery everywhere was so great that mothers speedily measured their children — size of head, width of shoulders, length of leg, size of collar, chest and hip measurements, enclosing with these, at my request, a rough drawing of each child's foot, for the French shoe measures are quite different from ours, and I feared to make mistakes.

In this way I gained time, for the transport of goods from England was still a lengthy business. When the cases did come — and I prayed like a steam-engine that they might arrive so that I could distribute them over a vast area before Christmas — I should be able to go straight ahead with the sorting, measuring and distribution of the eight thousand garments and three hundred pairs of precious shoes, not to mention cots, mattresses and blankets. I had good friends in L'Entr'aide of London by whom all shipping was done, and fortunately the man in charge, Commandant Boury, was a competent "live wire." He, if anyone, would get those things across France in time, never ceasing to badger L'Entr'aide H.Q. in Paris till the cases were put on to the train.

In the intervals between interviews I strove to put my little "Sunset House" into its original state. John's books and mine, my linen, crystal, silver, brass and pewter had been stored in the flat of a friend near Grasse, with certain loved pieces of family furniture and a host of personal possessions. As she lives below the edge of the main road very near to the enormous American villa which the Germans used as headquarters, I had very little hope of seeing any of these things again — the silver and crystal had been packed in strong cases as for export, in order to transport them from "Sunset House," and all the Germans had to do was to label them BERLIN and send them to the Fatherland. I had done the packing for them before I left! That fact embittered certain moments when I thought of it in England.

But no! This faithful old friend had cleverly tricked the Germans by mixing my sheets, etc., with hers, arranging various *bibelots* of mine among her own possessions, and putting the packing cases in an end room with dust-sheets over them and my odd pieces of furniture piled anyhow on top of them. The room was purposely never dusted or swept, and on entering it one had the impression that it was full of unwanted junk. My friend had explained that she had never yet had time to furnish that room, and so had stacked the furniture there till she had leisure to arrange it. Underneath the pile of "junk" was the enormous mahogany brass-bound silver chest containing all our wedding presents, including the large silver rose bowl given to us by King George V. and Queen Mary, and the silver "Paul Lamerie" salver presented to John by his messmates in the *Medina* when he went to India with the King to write the story of the Durbar. These, with all our family silver, could have been stolen by anyone during those years of war, for whether by negligence or accident in transit the great chest was not even locked! It proved to be one of my friend's greatest anxieties all through those dreadful years. She was marvellous! Though lacking soap and all toilet necessities, for in the end every shop was depleted of its goods, she had never touched any of my surplus stores, which had been thrown into baskets and sent with the packing-cases after my departure. How she must have looked, and coveted, poor darling, yet she never touched a thing, though it would have comforted me so much to know that anything of mine could have lessened the hardships she and all my friends endured.

Since my return she was longing for the removal of all these things, that she might put her house in order and let her flat, and so I arranged for them to be collected by lorry, fetching crystal vases, lamps and fragile things myself later on when my own car arrived. The little Grey Pigeon was being driven from Paris by a member of the French Red Cross. I was so overjoyed to see her when she did arrive, with the seven-pointed stars painted upon her back and doors, that I actually kissed her dusty little nose. She had been driven as far as Paris with a convoy of ambulances and army lorries (I hope she was in the place of honour at its head) by the Quakers, and then the French Red Cross took her over and brought her South. The driver told me she had behaved beautifully all the way. *Of course* she did; she has never given me any trouble yet, bless her gallant little heart, thanks in great measure to the tender care given to her little interior by her clever godfather-mechanic, my old friend "Mr. Oliver."

Somehow I felt less lonely after the arrival of my little Grey Pigeon. We had crusaded together all through the war, and nearly always on the armchair seat next the driver had sat another loved and faithful little friend. She and I and The Blackness had been inseparables for six years, and to me she is not a car but a PERSON. We were to have many more adventures together and do much good work still in the then unknown future.

My possessions arrived from Grasse and formed a small mountain in the courtyard, where I left them for the time, lacking the courage to unpack nearly two thousand books, dust them, carry them upstairs and rearrange them on the shelves which line my studio and the corridor. But suddenly I was galvanised into activity by an announcement from Paris that one hundred and eight cases of clothes had been put on to the train for the South that day! Heavens! I must clear the courtyard before this fresh load of packing-cases arrived, and I feverishly set to work.

John's books and mine had always been the horror of every household removal we had made, also an annual labour when I dusted them all during our orgies of spring cleaning, and I knew how dusty and tiring the job would be. But it was a thousand times worse than I anticipated, for the conscientious packer, to economise every inch of space, had packed them according to the convenience of their size and NOT in series. The result was a neat and finished jig-saw puzzle; John's lovely little ancient editions of the classics were mixed with Roxburgh Club editions, my poets, military history, *and* the forty-six volumes of the complete works by Sir Walter Scott (who, for some reason, I *cannot* read). These were nearly my despair, for I kept on finding yet another volume in a different case. A heavy job, but at last it was all done, and my lovely family crystal from Waterford placed once again in the invisibly illumined alcoves in the hall and little salon. My dear "Sunset House" began to look like HOME again, with flowers arranged everywhere in the bowls and tall vases my dear friend had guarded so carefully.

As I opened cupboards and drawers which had been locked all through the war, I kept discovering what had now become priceless treasures — quarto scribbling blocks, typing paper, pencils, clips, soap — unprocurable things in France. There was even a pair of strong shoes that I had never worn, and yards of material which I had not had time to make into curtains. It was like having some wonderful birthday finding again these forgotten things, which seemed to me now like gifts of God.

Hardly had Margharita (purring loudly because the house now looked as once it had) polished the floors and furniture, and the packing-cases been removed by a kind peasant, than a huge lorry arrived at the front gate laden with the clothes and comforts for the children of Provence!

CHAPTER
FIFTEEN

Rich Chaos

Poor Margharita wrung her hands and groaned. Where would Madame unpack these cases? The garden had only just been cleared! And where put the contents of all those huge cases? Madame, having seen the work that her poor Margharita had put in to make the little house beautiful, steeled herself to reply: "In the hall and the salon and the guest-room and the loggia, but we must try not to overflow into the rooms upstairs." For once my Margharita looked rebellious.

"*La belle maison de Madame!*" she muttered, with angry tears in her eyes. All through the war she had longed for the moment when once again *les belles choses de Madame* should be displayed in their accustomed places and she in proud charge. That moment had, at last, come, and now Madame was going to fill the rooms with second-hand clothes, and *le bon Dieu* alone knew what else besides; and if the great loggia outside the front door was also used that would mean that the door must always be left open while Madame unpacked and sorted the things, and the wind would fill the rooms with straw and paper and sand from the courtyard. Poor Margharita broke her usual taciturn silence and became a voluble and ill-used Italian. It was terribly hard upon her, but I was not going to enjoy having my home turned into a clothes and comforts depôt either.

"Dear Margharita," I said very gently, putting my arm about her thin shoulders, "I *do* understand, and it is very cruel for you after all your hard work. We're both going to *hate* it, but after all, the beauty of the house matters nothing really compared with the joy the contents of those cases will give to so many of the miserable homes here. Think of poor little Madame X. with her six children in rags! I saw her yesterday, and her own poor feet were bleeding because her *pantoufles* are worn out and there are no more to be had. And there is Madame G., who is going to have a baby in a minute and no clothes to dress it in; no cot, no blankets, and she is very delicate." I enumerated various others known to her. "You and I, Margharita, are going to work as we have never worked before to help these *malheureux*, not only in our own village but in the whole Canton du Bar, and even farther afield. We must not think of ourselves for one minute, for the time is very short — and I think it will snow to-morrow. It is already the fifteenth of December, and every one is counting upon something to help and comfort them for Christmas. We must get these things unpacked, sorted and distributed by then — or at latest by the New Year, your great *Fête* here. You are going to help me, my Margharita; you have never failed me yet."

The expression of her great eyes was softened but still piteous.

"It is not only the house of Madame," she said in a

choked voice, "it is about Madame herself that I grieve. She is tired already and should rest. This work will kill her. Oh, I know the people here, they will leave Madame *no* peace — and I know my Madame; she will never refuse to see them and listen to them. I *know*, I *see* what it will be."

"But Margharita," I said, "you are not yet old; you cannot know the joy it is still to be needed — and needed desperately when you have reached the age of fifty-seven. Besides, what is the health of one woman if she can help the miseries of thousands?"

"Madame is precious to many. She is precious to *me*. And I cannot feed her as she should be fed while she is working so hard — there is so little food."

She fled down to the kitchen rather than let me see her break down.

"God's little finger will hold me up," I said to myself, as I climbed wearily upstairs.

The cases had arrived in beautiful condition banded with steel. I wished the dear carpenter in England who had worked with such enthusiasm to ensure their safe arrival could have seen them after their long journey. He would have been as proud of them as I was of him. Margharita and I battled with screwdrivers and every kind of tool, but those steel bands defeated us, and I had to send for the husband of old Marie in the village, who would sometimes do odd jobs. The only condition his wife made was that he should not be allowed to lift or drag those enormous cases, because he had something wrong with his inside.

"*Il a mal-là*," she explained, putting her hand on her

116

tumpkin. I promised her that Monsieur Marie should not be asked to do any heavy work, but only file through those steel bands which, if he liked, he could do while in a sitting position. He arrived next day, beaming with pride at being asked to help with *l'oeuvre de Madame*, and quite obviously bursting with curiosity to see the contents of those cases and to be the first to broadcast the news. He took off his coat to begin.

Before he started work I remembered to caution him on no account to try to shift those heavy cases, because his wife had told me about him, and I placed my hand on my tumpkin. To my unspeakable surprise and consternation, he whipped up his shirt and threw it over his head displaying a bare stomach. Pointing dramatically at his navel, he ejaculated, *"La! C'est là!"*

Has any other woman in the world, within three minutes of making acquaintance of a man, been so complimented?

I had never met Monsieur Marie before. He and his wife were evacuees from a distant town, but she had already helped Margharita in the house. When I had sympathised and proffered counsel, he began to work with a will. Soon the first lid was off, and as I pulled out armfuls of lovely warm pullovers, dresses, coats, the excitement of Margharita and Monsieur Marie knew no bounds.

"Ah! les belles belles robes! Pur laine! Quelle merveille!" chanted Margharita.

"Mais il-y-a des milliards de francs là dedans!" shouted Monsieur Marie, with goggling eyes.

To equalise weight, when packing, we had been

obliged to mix boots and shoes and heavy tins among the clothes. So that the contents of every case had once again to be sorted. All that afternoon the bell at the service entrance of the garden rang and rang, and every time it announced the arrival of yet another peasant mother from the village, who said she had heard that the cases of Madame had arrived, so had come up to see if she could help Madame to unpack them. Very transparent!

With eyes on stalks they stared at the stacks of lovely warm and pretty clothes I had begun to fold and to pile upon the long refectory table in the hall. They could not resist touching them any more than Margharita, a proud show-woman, could resist unfolding them, the better to display their glory to her thrilled audience.

"But they would cost too much for us," one little woman remarked to her. Whereupon Margharita laughed triumphantly as she told her that these were *gifts* from the English people to their friends in France.

"It is so, Madame, I speak the truth, don't I?" she almost shouted in her excitement, turning to me for confirmation of this, to them, amazing statement. Bedlam was then let loose and hay was made of things I had already arranged. This jumper would fit little Denise perfectly — those small knickerbockers were just the affair of little Paul, whose stern was positively visible through his present pair and no material left anywhere in the world with which to patch them, and even if a patch could be found, *who* possessed a needle? And the last reel of thread in Grasse had cost its purchaser one hundred francs. Impossible for the poor. Then someone spied a whole box full of needle cases and a large canvas bag filled with hundreds of reels of cotton, another with strands of *new* mending wool gifts collected by the women of the W.V.S. and by various women's institutes all over England. Then those poor mothers dissolved into silent tears. It was too beautiful — it was surely too good to be true. Margharita told them that in those cases were eight thousand garments, even real leather shoes — and SOAP, not only for their children but for all the children of Provence. She pointed a brown finger to the stencilled name of my fund on the lids and sides of the cases.

"Madame has collected money and these clothes and comforts for the children of Provence in memory of Mademoiselle Starr — our beloved Mademoiselle," explained Margharita. The tears ran faster down those thin white faces as that sacred name was mentioned. SHE had always helped the *malheureux*, why must she be taken from those who needed her so much? they mourned. Why — oh why?

Her poor substitute strove to change their sad thoughts by suggesting that she and Margharita should now equip these mothers with warm clothes for themselves and their children. Thenceforth chaos and eventually pandemonium. Another huge case was opened and its contents feverishly fished forth, dresses, shoes and pullovers tried on. Minds could NOT be made up — that dress fitted so well — but perhaps the coat and skirt over there, though not so pretty, was more practical. Those shoes were *chic* — but perhaps the brogues were more suitable and useful for a *mère de famille* on these rough mountain roads. They had a glorious day, and would have remained in my house

119

all night trying on everything already unpacked if, at eight p.m., Margharita had not firmly said that she must absolutely now cook the supper of Madame. Then, with apologies, they went after kissing me with violence on both cheeks and calling down upon me the blessings of heaven as they collected their chosen garments and went forth joyously chattering into the night.

CHAPTER
SIXTEEN

Hardship

That one afternoon taught me that if I were to get the mass of material sorted and distributed within the time-limit that I had set myself, I must refuse all offers of help from the women in the village and cope with it myself, aided very occasionally by Margharita when she was not walking for miles in search of food, queueing for rations, cooking, cleaning, searching for dropped olives or wild oats in the hedgerows to feed her hens, and doing all her other usual and self-imposed duties. So from early morning till late at night and sometimes into the early hours of the next day I unpacked, sorted and placed those eight thousand garments. My little green salon became the Baby Clothes Department, the divan was piled to the ceiling with thousands of tiny woollen coats, vests, pilches, bootees, mittens, belly-bands and shawls which, later on, I made up into layettes. Each bundle was rolled in one of the lovely gay cot-covers knitted by children of English kindergartens, who each contributed a square, a triangle or an oblong strip, sometimes embroidering a message in French for the baby who would receive it, or a little tricolour flag. I think the peasant mothers were more touched by these little patchwork quilts than by anything else. Inside each layette I included a cake of baby soap (sent by American friends) and a block of household soap, also a towel, some white, pink or blue mending wool and a face flannel. I filled a huge cupboard with these layettes, so that when a doctor gave me names of expectant mothers in his district I could immediately hand him the requisite number. The beauty of their contents reduced the recipients — sometimes even the doctors — to grateful tears. They had all lived in dearth and misery for so long.

Chairs and tables in the salon became loaded with little frocks, coats and knickers for babies up to three years old and little girls and boys up to five. Clothes for children in their teens, for women, and even a few suits for men, I placed in the hall in every available place. Even the great open fireplace was full of hats, caps, scarves and stockings, so that one had to poke one's head under the hooded chimney to see the top of the pile. No fear of soiling by soot, for it had been unused for so long in a country devoid of fuel.

The loggia became a shoe shop, hundreds of pairs of shoes displayed upon the enormous table, and the lids of empty cases while under the table were cases of mending materials, knitting wool, besides medical and surgical stores sent to me when Red Cross relief centres were disbanded after peace was declared. These were eventually sorted, and I filled small wooden cases with a selection of each precious thing to give to the overworked doctors of the neighbourhood, who had then no bandages, gauze, lint, syringes — in fact they had NOTHING. At the French Red Cross Dispensary in Grasse I found the poor nurse trying to give an injection with half a broken glass syringe. She tried to exclude the air with her thumb. The injection, which should have taken thirty seconds or so, took three-quarters of an hour, and was only achieved after four attempts. The patient fainted, and the nurse cut her thumb badly and had to be bandaged. The only available soap was the *ciment*. It was a mixture of sand and potash, with some ghastly ingredient which stank to high heaven, to hold it together. Such was the state of things in the winter of 1945. No wonder those in charge of hospitals, crèches and dispensaries became almost hysterical with joy and relief when they received these wonderful gifts. Besides all the public institutions, I was able to equip ten individual doctors. One of them wrote me a beautiful letter on behalf of them all, which I must quote here.

"Nous savons bien que nous pouvons jamais acquitter la lourde dette que nous devons, mais avec toutes nos forces nous essayerons d'être digne de nos amis Anglais dont vous êtes la grande ambassadrice."

(We know well that we can never repay the heavy debt that we owe, but with all our strength we shall strive to be worthy of our English friends whose great ambassadress you are.) The French (the real and true French) *DO* love us and are deeply grateful to us, so *DON'T* listen to mischievous propaganda which is ever trying to separate our nations. . . .

Measuring each garment to fit the requirements of every child on my list was a tremendous work. I went about with a centimetre measure hung round my neck. Fortunately, at this moment, an Austrian refugee living

123

in the neighbourhood asked if I could employ her as life was so hard and she had a sick husband. She made careful records of all the comforts given out and to whom they were given. In one village alone there were one hundred and eighteen necessitous families, all of them prolific. The clothes of each child we tied into a bundle and all the bundles into a big bundle, and all the bundles of all the families I put into my mattress cases and labelled them with the names of the villages. I ran out of string and had to go into Grasse to buy several balls of the French variety, which looked very strong and was enormously expensive, but, as I proved to my cost later, was made of paper. No one had any transport, so the delivery of my *ballots* must be made by me and my little Grey Pigeon. She would be overweighted and overworked, but I knew that she would never let me down, and she never did.

Snow began to fall and the house became bitterly cold. It blew through the open door into the hall and through the windows, which had to be left open to let out the asphyxiating fumes of naphthaline packed with the clothes. My "shop" in the loggia had to be rearranged, and all those shoes placed on the floor beneath the table. The pencil fell from my frozen fingers, and in one week I broke the frames of four pairs of spectacles, putting them on to read my lists and taking them off to cross the floor, finally dropping them from numbed and nerveless hands. At night I slept rolled in a cocoon of blankets, wearing most of my clothes, and even then I couldn't get warm, partly, I think, because I was empty inside.

The only fire in the house was in my studio, where

Margharita and I cowered in the evening over the olive twigs we had collected during the day. Very often we had to cook our little saucepan of soup over this fire when the electricity was cut and she could not make use of her new toy, the tiny electric cooker, that I had brought out for her. Electricity was severely rationed when at last it was re-connected. We had it for half an hour in the early morning, for an hour — eleven to twelve — so that *déjeuner* could be cooked, and sometimes for an hour in the evening. But there were days when there was no supply at all, and I was thankful that all through the war I had ordered a packet of candles with my weekly rations, for although I could not always get them, still I had collected quite a good supply to take to France. My old friend the wonderful grocer of my Sussex village did his best for me always, and I have never yet had time to tell him how I hoarded that last packet of biscuits he put into my hand for the journey when saying good-bye. With these and my last packet of English lump sugar I rationed myself very severely in that hungry land, and when I felt really faint I would suck a lump of sugar or eat *one* mouthful of biscuit.

Once, when Margharita had spared a little precious olive oil in which to toss the dried beans she had cooked for our supper, alone in my studio I actually — I will whisper this — licked my plate! The dark bread was too hard to sop up those drops of precious oil, and they must not be wasted. Oh, shades of Windsor Castle! Yes, my little loved Blackness was better where he was.

CHAPTER
SEVENTEEN

The Miracle of Meat

One day I was busily making up *ballots* alone in the loggia when the bell hanging outside the gateway of the courtyard clanged furiously, and went on clanging and clanging and clanging. As Margharita did not rush to answer it I realised that she must be down in the village. What a bore! A school teacher was arriving with a hand trolley in half an hour and, if uninterrupted, I had just time to complete my list so that he — or she — could trundle this *ballot* to Châteauneuf and save me that journey anyhow. Hoping that I could deal with this unseen person by merely yelling across the courtyard from where I stood, and continue my packing at the same time, I shouted, *"Qu'est ce qu'il-y-a? Qui est-là?"* The bell clanged again more violently, and a hoarse voice screamed excitedly, between clangs:

"Madame! (Clang!) *Il-y-a de la VIANDE!* (Clang! Clang!) *Il-y-a de la VIANDE.* (Clang! Clang!) *Ily-a-de la VIANDE!"* (CLANG! CLANG! CLANG!)

The miracle of meat being sold in the village after so many years when meat was scarcely seen! Madame Pagani, still wearing the same hat she wore when she and her husband sold me "Sunset House," had toiled up the mountain to announce to me this stupendous event. She did not want me to miss this rare treat. Of course I had opened my great doors to thank her for her kindness, but for once she did not linger, she was in far too great a hurry to get home and cook her bit of meat for her hungry family. Margharita reappeared very much later. She had seen the travelling butcher arrive and had queued for two hours with a mob of excited peasants to obtain our four square inches of rhinoceros.

What a contrast was my present life in Provence to that of the old happy days when Emilia and I went to market together in *Désirée*, my great Fiat saloon car, and bought the weekly supplies: a luscious cut of lovely tender meat, fresh fish for supper, perhaps a plump Brésse chicken, a great slice of Brie cheese, a jar of whipped cream, and two kilos of golden butter sent from Normandy in a tub and scooped out liberally to all comers. Reasonable prices, no rationing in that land of peace and plenty which once was France!

Now — nothing for sale in the markets save a few dried-up vegetables — 18 francs for one skinny leek — and perhaps a slab of *morue* (salted cod), which hung despairingly from a hook, its surface covered with flies. I preferred to be hungry (or shall I say hungrier?) than eat this loathsome fish which perfumed the whole house when Margharita cooked some for herself.

Nearly everything in our kitchen garden had failed through drought, and the land was impoverished for lack of manure which now fetched a fantastic price. Margharita came to me one day brandishing a pick-axe, and told me ruefully that she had been trying for an hour (and had mercifully failed) to break open the septic tank of Madame down in the olive grove. Its contents would be precious for the garden of Madame. . . !

My beautiful septic tank, created at enormous cost by a firm in Nice. It stood like a whited sepulchre on the lowest terrace, and its interior chambers were the pride of its creator, who had fortunately sealed it with the solid cement that had defeated Margharita. Although invisible to the house, I had nevertheless caused it to be turfed over, and it looks like a hidden gun-emplacement of yesterday. Thank heaven it was strongly built, but Margharita was bitterly disappointed that I could not (*she* thought would not) tell her how to open it.

Another thing that worried her was the army of rats. So far they had not entered the living-rooms, but they had held high carnival in the loft, eaten her baby rabbits and much of the fruit crop, climbing up the vines to devour the grapes and running along the branches of the fig trees. She had implored me to bring back with me from England some form of rat exterminator, and I had brought the poison recommended by the Ministry of Agriculture. You strewed good oats near the rat runs for three days to allure and give them confidence, and then you put down real poison which, I was assured, they would eat likewise — with fatal results. I followed the directions carefully, using a long spoon to spread the oats so that the rats should not smell the touch of human hand. Every morning of those three days I visited the rat-runs. Not an oat was to be seen.

They had taken the bait. So far, so good. Now for the poison.

The next day I visited the runs filled with expectation. THE POISON WAS UNTOUCHED.

These being Provençal rats, I suppose the elders of the tribe sniffed the concoction, then tapped their old noses and smiled. After which they warned the younger members not to touch that poisonous stuff placed where they had found the delicious oats on the three previous nights. All I had done was to fatten my rats with good English grain. Life was hard and lonely, the intervals of pause filled only with amusing (to me) incidents such as these. No electricity to run the wireless; letters took an interminable time to come; we hardly ever saw the one sheet of newspaper that was printed, and, as I was the first of the English colony to arrive, when the telephone rang, it was invariably a call of distress from some French doctor or *oeuvre*. My ration of petrol, forty litres per month, would scarcely be enough for the distribution of the clothes and comforts unless I loaded my Pigeon to the roof and combined several deliveries in one day — or night — so that visits to Cannes or Nice were impossible. For sport I knocked snow from the branches of overladen cypress trees out of doors and crumbled the *mégauds* (stub ends) of my vanishing-in-smoke English cigarettes, rolling the tobacco thus gained into other very nicotiney cigarettes with the cheap gadget possessed by every peasant. Doubtless soon I should get to the point of making cigarettes from the stubs of stubs — and then get nicotine poisoning. But a cigarette seemed to dull appetite, and that was a blessing in those days.

In a life such as I have described, when to change our thoughts we were dependent upon what village gossip Margharita culled, the death of a very rich and miserly old woman who hated every one except her dog, and had never been known to alleviate the miseries of the poor around her with her vast wealth, shook the whole neighbourhood. And when it became known that she had bequeathed no less a sum than one thousand francs to anyone — *anyone* and every one — who would follow her to her grave, the excitement of the population became intense. Bequests were left also to convents and to priests who would pray for her soul. Ignored in life she had evidently been determined that all honour should seem to be given to her in death, and that her *pompes funèbres* should exceed in grandeur anything ever before seen in that line.

Hundreds upon hundreds of peasants from outlying villages trudged for miles to join in the funeral procession of this woman whom they had never even seen. Six members of one family were present, netting the good sum of six thousand francs for their walk up the mountain to the cemetery, at the gate of which stood a man with a notebook and fountain pen to inscribe the names and addresses of all beneficiaries.

The director of a large orphanage heard of the "bribe" and actually telephoned to the Mayor of Grasse to ask him if he did not think it a good idea that all the forty orphans should attend the funeral and so earn forty thousand francs for their upkeep, but the Mayor, a man of great integrity, cut into this unpleasant conversation with an angry, "*NON — c'est vilain ça, ce n'est pas joli d'exploiter la mort.*" So that was that, and the orphans did not join in the procession, to the deep mortification of their director, who could not bear to see good money lost for a scruple.

Margharita, also, was deeply chagrined because although she was one of the first to hear of the death of Madame X., was ignorant of the sequel, and so lost one thousand francs which, to her frugal mind, represented riches.

Shortly after the great day of the funeral one of the municipal councillors of our village came to me to solicit aid for a family living in squalor in one of the rooms of the defunct woman's enormous house. The family consisted of a mother and three children, who all slept on — not *in* because there were no blankets — one single bed. The old grandmother slept upon straw on the ground. They were evacuees from Marseille — a drunken brute of a husband had turned his family out of doors, and they had wandered into our district and pleaded with Madame X. to let them occupy a garret in her many-roomed house. She consented to RENT them a room if they would help with her farm, the olive-picking and the harvesting of grapes from her acres upon acres of vineyards, and there they had lived for years in the same house as that rich old woman whose many rooms contained beds and blankets enough to equip a small hospital. Think of the joy and comfort she could have given with all that useless wealth!

With bitterness in my heart I delivered cots and clothes for the children, a mattress for the poor old grandmother, and blankets and food for all; and as I looked at the great family tomb Madame X. had caused to be constructed on a wooded knoll of her vast domain, in which her own pitiful remains were now lying, I offered up a little prayer of my own for her poor mean soul.

CHAPTER
EIGHTEEN

The Belt and the Man

Margharita had grown restless and discontented of late, quite unlike her usual self. I put it down to her anxiety for the health of her old father in Italy, who had been failing for some time and never ceased to ask for her. But to enter Italy from France had become almost impossible since the war, and for months and months Margharita had been visiting Consuls and Mairies and battling against the new restrictions and formalities. She had to get her mother to visit their family doctor and ask him to give a certificate concerning her father's health. This had to be stamped officially by the *Maire* of her home village, who then must send it to the *Maire* of Opio, who in his turn sent it to the Italian Consul in Marseille, who must send it to Paris. . . . And so it went on. If her father had been dangerously ill he could have died and been buried many months before Margharita's permit to travel arrived. It was enough to fray the nerves and temper of anyone, but not only was Margharita irritable and sulky but — she had become queer — very queer. Suddenly at ten o'clock at night she would ask me if she could walk to Magagnosc — about three kilometres away — to post a letter.

When I suggested that Opio post office was nearer she expressed fears that the post box there might not be cleared, Madame Julien, who was in charge of it, had so much to do. Then I was asked in rather a defiant tone if I objected to her taking a moonlight walk. Did I think her mad?

No, pre-eminently sane, I assured her, but expressed fears that as she had been on her legs all day the long walk would tire her. Otherwise the frosty air could do no one anything but good.

Then one evening, returning home from her day off duty, she entered my studio with sparkling eyes and asked me, with unusual animation, if I would like to see something she had bought for herself. This was so unusual an event (for Margharita dressed soberly in black and never spent anything upon herself) that I expressed excitement and unbounded curiosity to see her purchase.

She untied a small parcel and displayed to my astonished stare a wide scarlet silk belt, hand-painted with Spanish ladies in dancing postures brandishing yellow fans and gay troubadours playing guitars.

Margharita had suddenly gone mad at the age of forty-five, or — and here a sudden cold chill came over me — that belt was designed to encircle a waist which, in its turn, would be encircled by a man's arm. That belt positively provoked encirclement. . . .

Now the moods and restlessness, the night walks to the post office, and the agony of frustration when her papers did not come for that journey to Italy were explained. Margharita disappointed in youth by the man of her choice had since, happily for me, turned against the sex. But now I feared that she was slowly revolving towards it again.

Well, I had been afraid that I should not always be able to keep such a treasure, but it seemed very hard that this should come upon me now. Without her I should be lonely and desolate indeed.

With forced enthusiasm I admired that fatal belt, and was then asked if I would allow her to go again to the town next day to try to find some kind of material to back it, for the red silk was only mounted upon cardboard. Reluctantly I gave permission, although I could ill spare the time to do Margharita's work as well as my own, for, with no transport, the walk to Grasse and back and the time taken to find what she sought would mean that she would not return home till late. Surely she would at least prepare some food to leave for me, as in old days, before starting on this second frivolous excursion.

But no! Next day, after sending up my early morning coffee in the service lift, Margharita vanished till nightfall, leaving nothing prepared, and I coped with cooking and the feeding of her hens and rabbits, answered bells, interviewed doctors, school teachers and peasants, and had a very busy day. I was too exhausted at night to take a very great interest in the strip of yellow cotton Margharita had found to back her belt, two scarlet pre-war bootlaces to lash it to her form through yellow eyelets bought from a cobbler, the remains of useless luxury stock and bought at exorbitant prices. Oh, certainly there must be A MAN in Italy.

The next day the post brought Margharita's visa for

Italy. She could start at once. She broke it to me that she would be gone for at least a month, perhaps more, for she had not been home for so long, and the journey (though paid for by me) was so expensive.

Well — I must try to manage somehow in her absence, though with the mass of stuff I still had to distribute this visit of hers to Italy could not have been worse timed. Even her two days of absence had tired me, and now I must face life without her for from four to six weeks. My spirit quailed. It was the beginning of the end, and secretly I wondered if she would marry in Italy and never return. That scarlet belt waved before my mental vision like the danger signal it was.

In Margharita's absence old Marie, the refugee, came up daily for an hour or two, found food — somewhere — for the hens and rabbits and for me, but for the rest of the day I was quite defenceless, for it is impossible to say that you are not at home when you open the door yourself. And the peasants, soon hearing that my watch-dog had gone and that they now had Madame completely at their mercy, never ceased to ring the bell for admittance to her — and the wonderful treasures she had brought from England. In addition to all this, Margharita's pet hen chose that moment to go broody, an event we had waited for with impatience, for we wanted to increase our poultry and get more life-saving eggs. So it fell upon me to find a peasant who could sell me a sitting of eggs, and the care of the broody lady when she was enthroned upon them; for she suffered from an excess of maternal instinct and had to be taken off her nest at intervals, by force, to eat and drink.

I had also been enjoined to look after Margharita's hideous lady cat, recently procured and greatly loved. Would Madame please see that "Tigrette" was always safely indoors at night, for cats — to kill rats — were now so precious that if allowed out at night "Tigrette" might be stolen.

Need I tell you that during Margharita's absence "Tigrette" became amorous, like her mistress, and absented herself during those days for frivolous reasons in like manner. She only appeared for an occasional meal, when she always evaded capture. At night I yelled myself hoarse calling "Tigrette! Tigrette!" but never a yowl did I get from her — in reply every male cat in the neighbourhood yowled in chorus with me and aided in the search. There could only be one end to this adventure. Margharita would not find "Tigrette" as she left her, and if she tarried long in Italy she might find more Tigrettes than she expected.

When I could bear this condition of things no longer, the baby chickens being due to arrive in a week's time, I had the inspiration to send Margharita a long telegram announcing their imminent arrival (she did not even know that one of her hens was sitting), and the fact that "Tigrette" was *enceinte* and that we all missed her terribly. If that didn't bring her back, nothing would.

Thank heaven it DID and — for the moment — no fatal ring was on her finger, and no word was spoken to me concerning approaching nuptials. But exaggerated care over her toilet and the fumes of Eau-de-Cologne issuing from her bedroom assured me that the danger was not past. The matter was brought to a head after several residents in the neighbourhood had sympathised with me over the imminent loss of my *bonne*. When I expressed surprise my informant invariably clapped his or her hand over the mouth as though to prevent further indiscretions escaping. Hurt to the quick that my Margharita seemed to have confided in every one else, I tackled her one evening.

"Margharita, is it true that you are going to leave me? Several people have expressed sympathy with me because of your approaching marriage. It hurts Madame to be apparently the only one in Opio who knows nothing about it."

She crimsoned, and for a moment her great eyes blazed dangerously. Before she could speak, I went on:

"Surely you know that all I want is your happiness — because I love you and can never repay you for all your fidelity. It will be a great grief to lose you, but if it is for your happiness — and every woman is happier in a little home of her very own and a man to look after her — I could not think twice of my own comfort. So tell me all about it, Margharita."

Then, in broken sentences, she told me that there *was* a man — but nothing was decided. She was so happy and comfortable with me; it nearly broke her heart to think of leaving me and her lovely little home here, for, after so many years, she felt that it *was* her home in France.

"But your people and your heart are in Italy, my Margharita, and in your own little house there with 'Monsieur Margharita' you will surely be happier still," I said.

Then came blinding enlightenment. "Monsieur Margharita" lived IN OPIO. He was an Italian mason. He was unpopular because, finding no work in France during the war, he had volunteered to go and work for the Boche in Germany. He had been *bien deçu*. Also he had had a mistress who was now in prison for five years for collaborating with the Germans. She had made him miserable, *le pauvre*, and he was well rid of her. But it was because Margharita knew that Madame had worked for the Resistance and could not approve of this man that she had never dared to confide in Madame. And anyhow nothing was settled — probably never would be, his character terrified her, for *"il s'allume comme une allumette"* and his temper was violent. But he was mad about her and would not leave her in peace. Besides, he was a spendthrift, had never saved a penny and had no home. He lived in three hired rooms in a ramshackle building with no water, not even a kitchen sink. She was used to the comfort of her own pretty bedroom and private bathroom — how could she endure such discomfort at her age? A young girl would be more adaptable.

Nevertheless she eventually decided that to have a man for her very own was worth the hardships she might have to endure, but it needed a violent scene in the Italian manner to make up her mind. I was in bed with high fever after an injection one wet and stormy night, and Margharita, with the world's worst cold in her head and throat, was shutting up the kitchen for the night, when I heard a man's urgent voice in the courtyard below my window. It became more and more voluble and excited. I could distinguish no words, but never before have I heard such a flooded stream of Italian. It poured, without doubt, over my poor Margharita, whose muffled interjectory monosyllables seemed to increase rather than to dam it. It seemed to flow on for hours, and as its volume increased so did my fever. Ought I to go down and interfere in what was none of my business — yet so vitally concerned me? No, it would upset Margharita all the more and certainly enrage this madman.

After an hour had passed I heard steps ascending towards my room, and presently a distraught Margharita appeared to ask me if she might go for a walk and strive to calm this man who was sending her mad, disturbing Madame, and would not be silent nor go away.

"But, Margharita, it is pouring with rain! How can a man who professes to love you ask you to go for a walk with him in such weather, when you have that terrible cold?"

She shook her head mutely and went out. A few minutes later I heard the kitchen door close and the sound of their voices growing fainter in the distance. It was then ten o'clock.

Fevered, and miserable for my Margharita, I lay awake for hours, hearing only the wail of the winter wind and the sound of the torrential rain gushing down the water-pipes and cascading into the *bassin*. At one a.m. I heard stealthy steps in the courtyard and then dragging steps coming upstairs. Margharita had returned and gone straight to her bedroom.

The next morning she appeared in my room looking

more dead than alive, and I said quietly: "Well? Is it all settled?"

It was. They were to be married as soon as possible. Then she told me that she had threatened to run away to Italy if he badgered any more, and he had forced her to give him her passport so that that was now impossible. Afterwards they had walked and talked and talked and walked until they found themselves outside the place where he lodged. He had dragged her inside and bolted the door, threatening to shoot her and then himself if she did not consent to marry him. Or he would keep her there all night, ruin her reputation and send Madame a note in the morning. She had reasoned, he had argued, he had cried and she had wept. But the outcome of it all was that they were now affianced and would like to be married, if it suited Madame, on 28th December — the anniversary of the Massacre of the Innocents. Truly an appropriate date.

*My poor Margharita!

*This marriage took place nearly two years ago, and thanks to Margharita's thrift and strength of character, and the man's very real devotion to her, it has proved to be a very happy one.

CHAPTER
NINETEEN

Relief Work and
Fêtes de Noël

As Christmas approached my activities became more and more hectic. The rain turned to snow, and the tortuous mountain roads became slippery and even more dangerous than in their natural state. I had no chains for my little Grey Pigeon, and when it was actually snowing, frequently had to dismount to free the clogged wind-screen wiper from snow. Often it took me so long to reach a village objective on some mountain peak that when I had finished distributing comforts my Pigeon and I were benighted, and I *hated* driving in the dark, particularly because one of the headlights functioned only intermittently and sometimes not at all. The Quakers who drove her to Paris for me had noticed that my little car had "a short," and had promised to revise the whole electric system before they started. Overworked as they were, with the whole convoy of lorries to supervise in like manner, they had evidently not had time to do this — and now *I* had none to spare. Garages in France in 1945 lacked mechanics and material. They would keep her for weeks and then probably return her still in a one-eyed condition. So I continued to take these risky drives, and the wonder is that I am still alive to tell this story. How I longed for a sturdy MALE helper to load my car before starting — oh, the difficulty of hoisting huge *ballots* over the bucket seats of a Baby Austin that had only one door a side! And, oh, their terrible weight on the back when climbing up broken stairways to the attics of ancient buildings where the very poor always seemed to live. And the French string securing the openings of my sacks! Often it would burst just as I had toiled up to the top flight, sometimes in pitch darkness, and boots, shoes, clothes, soap and tins of food, cascading down the stairs, must be painfully collected by the light of an electric torch.

When this first happened, at the end of a long day, I sat down on the top step and wanted to break down and sob with fatigue — and RAGE. Then my sense of humour reasserted itself as I realised how ridiculous I must look, a grey-curled old witch trying to play the picturesque part of *"Maman Noël"* (the name the children of Provence instantly gave me when I appeared at Christmas in the place of *"Papa Noël"* with sacks of treasure on my back), sitting on the stairs in the darkness surrounded by all these miscellaneous objects, and I laughed till I cried instead.

I felt very shy when first entering these poor homes; for the French are a proud people, and since the war they were hypersensitive, and would bitterly resent the least suspicion of patronage. For this reason French officials had rightly been careful about whom they allowed to do relief work. I had lived in France for a long time and my

143

love and understanding of the French was well-known, but to these families in outlying villages I was a stranger who might seem unwarrantably and unpardonably to intrude upon their privacy — and poverty. Had I been able to tell the priest or doctor who had given me their addresses the hours at which I should be doing my distributions in their district, they would gladly have accompanied me and given me an introduction. But I had to fit in journeys between the unexpected visitors to "Sunset House" who came with the recommendation of their mayor, doctor or priest, and had to be equipped on the spot. Such pitiful people — like the little post-mistress who had to tramp with her mail-bag in broken sandals, and with only a thin cotton rag worn as a shawl to cover her torn cotton blouse. She delivered my letters, crying with sheer misery; she literally danced away clad in a woollen jumper, a tweed coat and skirt, thick woollen stockings and solid leather brogues on her feet. *"Qu'on est BIEN là-dedans,"* she chanted, as she trotted off, refreshed by a glass of hot wine.

Then there were the children of an orphanage — their mothers dead and their fathers shot in the Resistance or collapsed in German prison camps. They were all herded to my door in their rags of clothes, their feet bare in the snow. Oh, the joy of dressing them warmly and shoeing their poor little feet! Since then I have been adopted as official *"Marraine,"* and whenever I pass that orphanage a rabble of *filleuls* and *filleules* rush out and force me to stop my car with their shrieks of *"Marraine! Marraine! Marraine!"*, their small bodies impeding my passage. They swarm on the running-boards fighting with each other to get my first kiss through the windows; they even scramble on to the bonnet and try to open the windscreen to embrace me. Warming and lovely to a desolate heart. So that you see it was quite impossible ever to fix a day or hour for distant distributions. I had to go when I could, and then explain myself to those whom I visited. The first time, as I had feared and anticipated, I was greeted on entering by a hostile stare which seemed to say, "Who are *you* to DARE to intrude upon our misery?"

I asked the occupants of that poor room to forgive my intrusion and to accept these gifts from English friends who knew how terribly they had suffered and were anxious to help them. For myself, I told them that in collecting and distributing these gifts I was trying to repay a small part of the debt I owed to my French friends for the happiness and hospitality I had received from them for so many years.

Then their expressions softened, and soon changed to amazement and awe when they saw the contents of the *ballots* which, magically to them, contained all the clothes they had lacked, and clothes which *fitted* them. I was charged to thank their unknown English friends. They were so touched that the English who had suffered so much themselves should make such sacrifices. I told them that one little girl of a school to which I had appealed had sold her precious bicycle to send the money to help the children in France, and that I had received five shillings from a very poor mother, one shilling for each of her five children who had had the luck to be born in England.

They listened in rapt silence, then murmured, *"C'est beau ça!"* I think so too. Very, VERY beautiful.

With Christmas so near I was very thankful for the odd toys, bags of sweets, bead necklaces, books and hair ornaments that some of my generous contributors had poked into odd corners of their huge parcels, because, for the first time since the occupation, the French had decided to celebrate Christmas properly, if only in the humblest manner. The school teachers of every village school had been striving for weeks to coach the children to act little plays — a tiring and disheartening job because no child can memorise much when its whole mind is concentrated upon its pathetic empty tumpkin. Another problem was to find costumes for these plays and tableaux, but every Frenchwoman is clever at contriving something out of very little, and I was able to help with odd bits of material from my cases, and the silver paper and coloured tissue with which my dear unknown British helpers had sometimes wrapped their gifts.

There would be Christmas trees — *Arbres de Noël* — even though there was nothing to hang upon them except silver- and gold-painted fir cones, and tiny lamps made of snail shells with little wicks floating in precious oil. The men of the villages went up into the higher mountains to cut and bring down fir trees, and messengers, with eyes bulging, came daily to my door to see if Madame could produce anything for their *Arbre de Noël*. In a country denuded of everything this was not difficult, for gloves, caps, scarves and oddments from my stores made lovely presents for children who, in the old days, would have disdained anything useful and appreciated only toys. The most exciting of all gifts were cakes of toilet soap, for the children born during the war had never seen soap that FOAMED when put in water. They had only known sandy blocks of "ciment" that scoured the skin from their poor little faces when their mothers scrubbed them too vigorously. Their excitement over this soap that foamed gave me an idea. I had been warned that the mothers might not be able to resist confiscating these precious cakes and selling them for an enormous price in the black market. So when I presented each school with a piece for every child, I suggested that the school teachers should tell them to run away at once and wash their hands with it in the school basins to see how beautifully it FOAMED. This was always done; it caused untold excitement, and I gained my point. Cakes of soap, once used, cannot be sold into the black market.

My greatest problem now was how I was going to attend the various Fêtes de Noël to which I had been invited, for I had contributed either a *goûter* (tea), items of costume for the plays, or gifts for the Christmas tree. Some of the villages had chosen the same day for their fête, the most popular dates being 23rd December and Christmas Eve. All of them were to start early in the afternoon, and were to end with a surprise for Madame. She knew already that this surprise would be *le hymne Anglais*, our National Anthem, sung in English as a compliment to Madame *"et sa noble Nation."* Had she not heard the children, hot from school, trying to sing it as they wound their way down the mountain paths towards home? The school teachers had been trying to instil this tune and those strange words into the heads of their pupils for the past two months and, if the person for whom all these efforts had been made failed to put in an appearance, bitter indeed would be the disappointment of the children and their teachers. Somehow I must visit all the Fêtes, even if the National Anthem had to start the proceedings, or interrupt them in the middle if I found that I could not stay for the end.

Two of the villages had chosen the same day and the same hour and, as they sent their invitations well ahead of time, I was able to warn one that I would come for the first part of the programme, but must then rush off in order to be present for the second half of the other Fête: in this way each village could arrange its programme so that I did not miss the star items.

The audience of the first, packed into the school hall, was almost purely peasant, the proud mothers and fathers of children taking part in the play. I was placed on a chair in the front row flanked by two *Curés*, a fat and a lean, and the village mayor.

We started the proceedings with *le hymne Anglais*, which was rather painful both for me and the performers. I feared that my elastic smile of surprise and delight must soon turn wry if more than one verse were attempted. All the eyes of the singers were fixed upon my face to see how this great "surprise" affected me.

Then came a fairy play, one of the most touching and pathetic things I ever saw — pathetic because the Fairy Queen was attired in a white flannel nightgown with a silver paper star in her hair. The Fairy Prince

148

had a doublet composed of red paper and a tricorne hat of the same material. He wore his own patched corduroy breeches and clumping wooden-soled boots in which he had trudged many mountain miles in the snow to play to this enthralled audience. There was a chorus of trumpeters with cardboard trumpets and tabards, but their nether parts also were clad in their own multicoloured patched shorts, while wooden sabots or sandals covered their poor little feet. In response to a wave of the Fairy Queen's wand an "American cousin," wearing a straw boater, suddenly appeared upon the scene and put everything right — perhaps an addition to the original script and intended as a compliment to a valued ally. Anyway, in the manner of that rich and generous ally he financed the poor heroine in her poverty and distress, thereby rendering her even more attractive to Prince Charming who, after stumbling over the cardboard sword which had swung between his legs, fell upon his knees and, fumbling in his breeches pockets produced a red heart made of tin which he presented to the Princess amid the thunderous applause of the audience, the fat old *Curé* shouting himself hoarse with excitement. After which *le hymne Anglais* was sung once more. Madame complimented everybody on a wonderful performance and, leaving them to enjoy the feast England had provided, drove to the Opio school.

Here the hall was packed. The Christmas tree sparkled in one corner of the platform, with all the gifts lying in a heap at its foot. Every inhabitant seemed to be there and all in happy mood. The curtain was just about to go up on the second part of the programme — I had timed things well, it seemed.

It started with a Nativity play. The pretty little daughter of the mayor represented the Virgin Mary, and was discovered kneeling before the *Curé*'s prie-Dieu, borrowed from the church, peeping at the audience through fingers which were supposed to be covering her face. To her the Archangel Gabriel appeared clad in a night-shirt and flapping his arms to represent wings. She beamed at him, he being an old friend and playmate, then he flapped through the curtains which formed a backcloth, and which had been pulled aside by the willing hands of the many performers hiding behind them. There appeared then a chorus of angels all dressed in little summer frocks of pale blue, pink or yellow — sent to me from America and given with the English winter woollens I had provided. On the angels' heads were wreaths of greenery, on their feet muddy shoes. They walked in procession round and round the stage, flapping their arms rhythmically up and down singing a latin chant (conducted by the *Curé*, whose empurpled face and fat tumpkin were plainly visible through a gap in the curtains), nodding and beaming at all their friends and relations in the audience. I remarked to the mayor that death would lose all its terrors if every one were sure that they would be greeted by such cosy smiling angels on the Other Side.

The tableau following showed St. Joseph (the small son of the post-mistress, very far from saintly and a great favourite of mine) having the greatest trouble with his semicircular beard, which was merely attached by an

150

elastic round his head and one moment jumped up into his eyes, was tugged down into its rightful place and immediately shot up under his nose. He finally captured it and held it tightly in his teeth so that it formed beard and moustache in one. Next to him were the Virgin Mary and the Holy Child, a lovely little boy with a gilded cardboard halo attached to his head, sitting, clad only in a skimpy vest, inside a washing basket filled with rushes. He sat with hand raised to bless us while the chorus of cosy beaming angels surrounded him, singing a Christmas hymn. The curtains were dragged together, and pulled open again for a final curtain. Every one on the stage bowed and beamed to thunderous applause. This was too much for the baby representing the Holy Child. Why should *he* have to sit still, holding his position with hand upraised blessing us all when every one else on the stage was bowing and smiling? He tried to scramble out of his basket-cradle, stood on its edge, overturned it and fell with a bump upon his little stern amid the spilled rushes. Before the curtains could be dragged together I saw the horrified face of the old *Curé* peering through a hole in the backcloth. It parted in the middle to admit all the children who had no part in the play, but provided a hidden (?) chorus behind the scene. (A line of muddy sabots, seen from below the hem of the backcloth, had already warned us of the presence of an invisible choir.)

After this there was a *Pas Deux* by two divine, fat babies; they were little more. They came on to the stage, waved plump arms, raised stocky bare legs into the air one after another, lost their balance, rolled around shrieking

151

with laughter, and finally, clutching each other round the neck for support, rocked together until they collapsed in a chuckling heap upon the floor to the roars of joy of the audience. I laughed till I cried. It was a wonderful impromptu performance and entirely their own idea. Only babies of a Latin country could be so entirely lacking in self-consciousness, or so bursting with *joie-de-vivre*. And it was a relief to see at least two healthy children in this land of malnutrition.

When every one had applauded and laughed till they were tired, the mayor approached me and held up his hand to enjoin silence. Then he made a very touching little speech in which he asked me to convey the thanks of all their hearts to the generous friends in England and America who had given them such joy and comfort. He asked for three English cheers for *"Maman Noël,"* who had brought these lovely gifts. Then at his signal there burst forth the strains of our National Anthem sung from really grateful hearts. So, after a *goûter* of hot chocolate made with full-cream dried milk from America, meat pies, jellies, cakes and jam sandwiches provided by our Dominions, ended the *Fête de Noël*.

EPILOGUE
1947

Well, it is finished at last, YOUR book, and as you read the last chapter you will realize in some measure what joy and comfort your wonderful gifts have given in a land where no joy or comfort was to be found.

With your money Elisabeth Starr's little hospital of St. Christophe has been consolidated, repaired and repainted. It is now in perfect order, and has a completely new drainage system. Fifteen children have been loved and tended there this year. But those repairs cost me very nearly all the money I had collected, such are the fantastic prices in France to-day. My dream of enlarging the hospital and creating there a permanent relief centre for maimed and crippled children on the lines of Chailey in Sussex must still remain a dream. We cannot even afford to pay the running expenses of the hospital, and so we have handed it over to *Le Rayon du Soleil*, that magnificent *oeuvre* of the French which rescues homeless children, gives them a happy, healthy life, and finds homes where people will adopt a baby for their own. St. Christophe will be transformed into *a Pouponnière*, and, with the smaller cots, it will be possible to house from twenty to thirty children.

The little hospital stands on one of the loveliest sites in Provence, perched on the side of a mountain, facing south, surrounded by olive groves, its terrace overlooking a wonderful view of mountains, vineyards and the distant sea. Here these abandoned babies will thrive and grow into happy, healthy citizens of France, and you now know that the money you so generously gave to me for the Relief of the Children of Provence has, even though post-war conditions prevent me from realizing the dream you wanted to make for me a reality, been well bestowed.

The distributions of food will still go on, while you, my friends in the Dominions and America, continue to replenish my stores. My poor brave friends in England, *you* are so hard-hit to-day that you can no longer help in any way, but you have done your noble part.

The food situation in the South of France is still, as I write, desperately bad. Bread, when one can get it, is a mixture of maize and ground olive kernels, heavy and almost uneatable. While the rich ever seem to be able to provide themselves with black market food, the poor cannot even afford to buy their official rations, and our help is needed in every direction. France is a very sick country. Corruption and selfishness still go on, and FEAR makes the peasant farmer hoard what food he grows, or, if he can be persuaded to sell it, to ask an exorbitant price of his neighbours lest conditions become even worse and he and his family be left hungry and destitute.

Nevertheless, I have hope and faith that when she has passed through this dark post-war tunnel France may emerge once more into the light, for the true spirit of France is invincible. Even to-day, amid all the difficulties of life and its terrible discouragements, the French peasant can rise buoyantly above them. When with his beloved family he can forget the cares of the present and revert to the happy past which, please God, the future will one day resemble. This last story will illustrate my meaning.

Just before I left France once more (in July 1947) to convalesce in England after a major operation (the stones found in my extracted gall bladder have helped to construct an old wall in Provence), I was invited to the celebration of the golden wedding of Monsieur and Madame Pagani, who have both triumphantly overpassed the Biblical span of life allotted to man. The excitement of this coming event shook every branch and twig of the great family tree for weeks beforehand. Their son-in-law, a fair, stocky Provençal with wicked blue eyes, who was rebuilding a wall on my property which had land-slid after rains, confided to me that on the great day he and one other had planned to create *une chambre verte* outside their old *Mas* while *Papa* and *Maman* and all the rest of the family went to early Mass. Although I had lived so long in the country I had never seen or heard of a *chambre verte* and asked to be enlightened. It is a room, built outside the house, with the green-leaved branches of trees interlaced and lashed to bamboo supports so that in hot weather the family can feast, in shade, out of doors. Even the largest room of the Pagani farmhouse could not contain the complete family of thirty-six — four generations of Paganis — all seated at table at one time. Trestle-tables must be made, and their *chambre verte* must be the largest ever seen.

The ambition of the family was to have a notice of this great event and a description of its glories appear in the French newspapers. One of the sons intended to take a photograph of the complete clan feasting together in *la chambre verte*, and they all hoped that this picture would be reproduced in the centre of the newspaper article. This could then be cut out and framed for *les vieux*, so that the old people could look at it with pride and say, "Ha! Ha! We are not finished yet!"

My work has brought me into touch with several charming French journalists, and when Louis confided this hope to me I resolved that I would snaffle one of them for the afternoon so that he might see and record in print all that happened. My journalist was keen to accompany me to this anniversary *fête* — golden weddings, celebrating such fertility, are rare. He had no car, so I arranged to fetch him in mine, and carrying with me my offering, a glittering brass Benares bowl, we drove up the track leading to the farmhouse at about three o'clock.

Monsieur Pagani, such a handsome old man, though toothless, looked magnificent wearing a loose white linen shirt belted into baggy black trousers with a wide black belt studded with steel, a large black sombrero hat tilted at a jaunty angle over one eye, swaggered to meet us followed by Madame Pagani, her generous proportions upholstered in the sober black worn by all elderly peasants for both great and small occasions. I congratulated them both gaily, and presented my gift to Madame Pagani, who took it, clasped it to her ample bosom, and strode back to the house without a word of thanks. "You've given it and I've got it," I commented mentally, using the phrase

156

of my brother's little Tidoeng servant when presented with a gift.

Monsieur Pagani then led us into the huge *chambre verte* in which all the thirty-six members of his family were somnolently drinking liqueurs supplied by a son in the wine trade. They had eaten themselves to a sit-still, and were now lazily exchanging reminiscences and chaffing one another, the sunlight filtering through the green branches, casting an attractive tracery of shadow upon the gay dresses of the young girls and lighting up the green, red and golden liqueurs in their glasses like jewels. Every one looked happy and, for once, replete; for every member of the family had hoarded for months in order to contribute to the *déjeuner d'honneur* of this great festival.

Among those present I met many old friends. With pride Monsieur Pagani presented the members of his handsome family that I did not know, making sly introductory remarks which were sometimes embarrassing, as when he tapped significantly upon the tumpkin of a very pretty grand-daughter married the previous year, winked at me and said, *"Bientôt."* The laughing girl, not in the least abashed, informed me that her baby was due very soon. What fun if it were to be born here and now in the *chambre verte* on grandpapa's golden wedding day — that would make thirty-seven of his children here to-day!

Suddenly the strains of an accordion woke the company into activity. A professional *accordioniste* had been hired from Nice so that the young might dance. But it was the old who took the lead, and proved to be indefatigable. Monsieur Pagani opened the proceedings with the youngest and prettiest of his daughters-in-law; Mademoiselle's old gardener from the château, who had married Madame Pagani's sister, seized another pretty damzel and started circling, with a fixed and glassy stare, and with an energy and agility staggering in a man nearing eighty.

Louis came up to me and begged me to notice how "*correcte*" they all were in spite of the fact that they had all drunk well — oh, VERY well! — at the *déjeuner*. I asked him if their first sight of *la chambre verte* created in their honour had given the old people great joy. His answer was the widest of grins, a ducking of the head between shrugged shoulders, and a swift waggling of both hands, far more expressive than many words. He told me that the priest had given a special Mass for them all early that morning. The old couple had walked to the little mountain church three kilometres distant with such members of the family who were not building *la chambre verte* or making festal preparations in the kitchen. The old priest had made them kneel together on the altar steps as they had knelt on their marriage day so many years ago, and he had blessed them as he had blessed them then. No stranger had been present at this service, only THE FAMILY. "*C'était beau ça, hein?*" he asked me, and I nodded assent, having no words for the moment. Cries of "Louis! Louis!" called him from my side — they all wanted him to sing. He has a good light baritone voice and much of the clever low comedian about him, and can keep a peasant audience amused for hours. He now sang a duet with a female cousin who was never once in tune.

They had wine-glasses in their hands, and these were clinked at intervals, a rather tiresome tame little song. But when Louis had drained his glass at the end, the liquor inside it evidently woke him up, for he suddenly sprang upon the table with the agility of a cat and started a solo which made up in *verve* and innuendo for all that the duet had lacked. Perhaps fortunately I could not follow all of it, for it was peppered with *patois*, but when a Provençal starts singing about moonlight and lovers and deep green woods I stiffen, hold on to my seat and prepare for anything. Louis's song was filled with significant gaps, but these silent gaps were filled with gestures and a play of dancing devilish blue eyes. His wife looked faintly disapproving, for his gaze while singing caught that of one pretty relation after another, but never hers. However, with the tact of a practised *coureur des femmes*, when the song was finished he jumped down, gave his wife a smacking kiss on her lips and a slap on her behind, filled up her wine-glass and his own, drank her a silent toast accompanied by a wink, and then, his duty well and truly done, ran around flirting with the younger women of the community.

More dancing, and this time Louis bowed low before the English directress of Elizabeth's little hospital. Known and respected by all for the selfless devotion with which she and her friend and partner have tended the sick and crippled children — for love — for so many years, she was sitting bolt upright, clad in a clean striped cotton dress, not a hair out of place, her hands folded in her lap, her clear blue eyes dancing with amusement at the antics of the old people who were again dancing vigorously. A perfect type of good, straight Englishwoman who would prefer to die rather than shirk her duty or swerve one hair's breadth from her standard of justice, truth and integrity. Louis stood before her, a cheeky light in his eyes and his arms held out questioningly. To my immense surprise — and delight — she went into them, and in a moment was whirling around in a kind of mad polka. I was secretly jealous. She is two or three years my senior — and she was dancing with the rest. I adore dancing, but no one had asked me to dance.

When they all returned, breathless, to their seats I rallied Monsieur Pagani about this omission. He opened his black eyes wide, gasped like a fish, and then ejaculated, *"On n'a pas osé!"* One of the younger women, overhearing our remarks, tried to pacify me by reminding me that having recently been cut in half and sewn up again it would be the last imprudence to risk violent exercise. Perhaps she was right, but I still regret my inactivity.

The last dance while I was present (for they kept up their festivities far into the night, and for two days and nights afterwards) was danced to the strains of — what do you think? *TA-RA-RA-BOOM-DE-AY!* The great feature of this dance was that at the *BOOM* the man put his hands under the armpits of his partner and bounced her up into the air as high as he could. Many of the younger men succeeded in bouncing their girls right up to the roof of *la chambre verte* so that some of them got caught by the hair like Absalom, and returned to earth shrieking with laughter in a very dishevelled condition, disturbing the family dogs, cats, pigeons and ducks which ran about among the guests, sat upon the laps of seated observers or fluttered about the trestle-tables. All was happy noise and confusion. One of the sons, seated near me, boasted of the happiness and unity of that large family. In all their married life *Papa* and *Maman* had never quarrelled. All the marriages of their children had been happy. "We are all good friends. We all help each other," he said.

As I prepared to take my leave with the journalist, who had not only taken the names of every one present and full particulars of their work for the Resistance, but had had the time of his life, Monsieur Pagani was dancing with his wife to that old familiar tune. At the word BOOM he strove to raise her majestic figure into the air — and failed. Then she grasped him under his armpits, tried to lift him — and failed. They fell upon each other's necks in paroxysms of laughter in which we and the whole family joined. The music ceased, I kissed and was kissed by both male and female members of that joyous family, and then both I and my companion walked away.

As we skirted a square stone receptacle sunk into the ground and filled with water in which a little white pig had been taking turns with the human babies of the clan to bathe and splash all the afternoon (to my great envy), I thought to myself that the recovery of poor France would be swift and sure if every man could say, "We are all good friends. We all help each other."

One great united and sustained effort — a joyous spirit of collaboration in its real sense, then

BOOM!

and lovely France will be lifted to the high place of honour among the nations which once she held — AND WILL HOLD AGAIN.

ISIS publish a wide range of books in large print, from fiction to biography. A full list of titles is available free of charge from the address below. Alternatively, contact your local library for details of their collection of ISIS large print books.

Details of ISIS complete and unabridged audio books are also available.

Any suggestions for books you would like to see in large print or audio are always welcome.

7 Centremead
Osney Mead
Oxford OX2 0ES
(01865) 250333

ISIS REMINISCENCE SERIES

The ISIS Reminiscence Series has been developed with the older reader in mind. Well-loved in their own right, these titles have been chosen for their memory-evoking content.

FRED ARCHER
The Cuckoo Pen
The Distant Scene
The Village Doctor

BRENDA BULLOCK
A Pocket With A Hole

WILLIAM COOPER
From Early Life

KATHLEEN DAYUS
All My Days
The Best of Times
Her People

DENIS FARRIER
Country Vet

WINIFRED FOLEY
Back to the Forest
No Pipe Dreams for Father

PEGGY GRAYSON
Buttercup Jill

JACK HARGREAVES
The Old Country

ISIS REMINISCENCE SERIES

MOLLIE HARRIS
A Kind of Magic

ANGELA HEWINS
The Dillen

ELSPETH HUXLEY
Gallipot Eyes

LESLEY LEWIS
The Private Life Of A Country House

JOAN MANT
All Muck, No Medals

BRIAN P. MARTIN
Tales of the Old Countrymen
Tales of Time and Tide

VICTORIA MASSEY
One Child's War

JOHN MOORE
Portrait of Elmbury

PHYLLIS NICHOLSON
Country Bouquet

GILDA O'NEILL
Pull No More Bines

VALERIE PORTER
Tales of the Old Country Vets
Tales of the Old Woodlanders

ISIS REMINISCENCE SERIES

BIOGRAPHY & AUTOBIOGRAPHY

NINA BAWDEN
In My Own Time

SALLY BECKER
The Angel of Mostar

CHRISTABEL BIELENBERG
The Road Ahead

CAROLINE BLACKWOOD
The Last of the Duchess

ALAN BLOOM
Come You Here, Boy!

ADRIENNE BLUE
Martina Unauthorized

BARBARA CARTLAND
I Reach for the Stars

CATRINE CLAY
Princess to Queen

JILL KERR CONWAY
True North

DAVID DAY
The Bevin Boy

MARGARET DURRELL
Whatever Happened to Margo?

BIOGRAPHY & AUTOBIOGRAPHY

MONICA EDWARDS
The Unsought Farm
The Cats of Punchbowl Farm

CHRISTOPHER FALKUS
The Life and Times of Charles II

LADY FORTESCUE
Sunset House

EUGENIE FRASER
The Dvina Remains
The House By the Dvina

KIT FRASER
Toff Down Pit

KENNETH HARRIS
The Queen

DON HAWORTH
The Fred Dibnah Story

PAUL HEINEY
Pulling Punches
Second Crop

SARA HENDERSON
From Strength to Strength

PAUL JAMES
Princess Alexandra

BIOGRAPHY &
AUTOBIOGRAPHY

EILEEN JONES
Neil Kinnock

JAMES LEITH
Ironing John

FLAVIA LENG
Daphne du Maurier

MARGARET LEWIS
Edith Pargeter: Ellis Peters

VICTORIA MASSEY
One Child's War

NORMAN MURSELL
Come Dawn, Come Dusk

MICHAEL NICHOLSON
Natasha's Story

LESLEY O'BRIEN
Mary MacKillop Unveiled

ADRIAN PLASS
The Sacred Diary of Adrian Plass Aged 37 ³/₄

CHRIS RYAN
The One That Got Away

J. OSWALD SANDERS
Enjoying Your Best Years

VERNON SCANNELL
Drums of Morning

BIOGRAPHY & AUTOBIOGRAPHY

STEPHANIE SLATER WITH PAT LANCASTER
Beyond Fear

DAVA SOBEL
Longitude

DOUGLAS SUTHERLAND
Against the Wind
Born Yesterday

ALICE TAYLOR
The Night Before Christmas

SOPHIE THURNHAM
Sophie's Journey

CHRISTOPHER WILSON
A Greater Love